NEW YORK REVIEW BOOKS
CLASSICS

THE TRUE DECEIVER

TOVE JANSSON (1914–2001) was born in Helsinki into Finland's Swedish-speaking minority. Her father was a sculptor and her mother a graphic designer and illustrator. Winters were spent in the family's art-filled studio and summers in a fisherman's cottage on the shore of the Gulf of Finland, a setting that would later figure in Jansson's writing for adults and children. Jansson loved books as a child and set out from an early age to be an artist; her first illustration was published when she was fifteen years old; four years later a picture book appeared under a pseudonym. After attending art schools in both Stockholm and Paris, she returned to Helsinki, where in the 1940s and '50s she won acclaim for her paintings and murals. From 1929 until 1953 Jansson drew humorous illustrations and political cartoons for the left-leaning anti-Fascist Finnish-Swedish magazine *Garm*, and it was there that what was to become Jansson's most famous creation, Moomintroll, a hippopotamus-like character with a dreamy disposition, made his first appearance. Jansson went on to write about the adventures of Moomintroll, the Moomin family, and their curious friends in a long-running comic strip and in a series of books for children that have been translated throughout the world, inspiring films, several television series, an opera, and theme parks in Finland and Japan. Jansson also wrote novels and short stories for adults, of which *The Sculptor's Daughter*, *The Summer Book*, *Sun City*, *Fair Play*, and *The True Deceiver* have been translated into English. In 1994 she was awarded the Prize of the Swedish Academy. Jansson and her companion, the artist Tuulikki Pietilä, continued to live part-time in a cottage on the remote outer edge of the Finnish archipelago until 1991.

THOMAS TEAL has translated Tove Jansson's *The Summer Book*, *Sun City*, and *Fair Play*.

ALI SMITH is the author of seven works of fiction, including the novel *Hotel World*, which was short-listed for the Booker Prize in 2001, and *The Accidental*, which won the Whitbread Award in 2005 and was short-listed for the 2005 Man Booker Prize.

THE TRUE DECEIVER

TOVE JANSSON

Translated from the Swedish by
THOMAS TEAL

Introduction by
ALI SMITH

NEW YORK REVIEW BOOKS

New York

THIS IS A NEW YORK REVIEW BOOK
PUBLISHED BY THE NEW YORK REVIEW OF BOOKS
207 East 32nd Street, New York, NY 10016
www.nyrb.com

First published by Schildts Förlags Ab, Finland as *Den ärliga bedragaren*
English translation first published in the United Kingdom in 2009 by Sort Of Books

Library of Congress Cataloging-in-Publication Data
Jansson, Tove.
 [Ärliga bedragaren. English]
 The true deceiver / by Tove Jansson ; introduction by Ali Smith ; translated by
Thomas Teal.
    p. cm. — (New York Review Books classics)
 ISBN 978-1-59017-329-9 (alk. paper)
 I. Teal, Thomas. II. Title.
 PT9875.J37A7513 2009
 839.7'374—dc22
                              2009040458

ISBN 978-1-59017-329-9
Available as an electronic book; ISBN 1-59017-684-9

Printed in the United States of America on acid-free paper.
10 9 8

INTRODUCTION

IN 1962 TOVE JANSSON published a story for children called 'The Spring Tune' featuring Snufkin, the peripatetic musician of the Moomin stories. "It's the right evening for a tune, Snufkin thought. A new tune, one part expectation, two parts sadness, and for the rest, just the great delight of walking alone and liking it." As he settles in to compose, he is disturbed by a small creature, a 'creep', which rustles out of the undergrowth, declares its admiration for the famous Snufkin, asks him a lot of questions and demands attention and comfort. Meanwhile the tune, which until then was forming itself out of the noises of forest and brook and the slow revelations of the season, disappears. Snufkin has to wait for it to come back.

Never underestimate Jansson, who never ever underestimates her reader. This story for eight-year-olds is a sharply pertinent discourse on the relationships between art, nature, fame and identity; a discussion of the place and role of the artist and of the mysterious sources of creativity. It could be said that everything she wrote is, in one way or another, about the creative interactions between art and reality or art and nature – and this latter happens to be the title of a story from a 1978 collection of short stories for adults, *The Doll's House* (the book she published directly before *The True Deceiver*).

The central character in 'Art and Nature' – an old caretaker responsible "for the whole of this big art exhibition and also for the forest" – finds himself refereeing a passionate argument between a husband and wife in a darkening sculpture park, about what a picture they've just bought actually represents. He sees that their picture is still wrapped up in its paper and string. He suggests that, to solve the disagreement, the couple simply leave it inside its wrapping from now on. "It's the element of mystery that's important, very important in some way." Simple as that. Then he ejects them from the park and goes off to his bed.

Tove Jansson was born an artistic child of bohemian Finnish artists. Her mother, Signe Hammarsten, was one of Finland's most well-known artists, designers and book illustrators; her father, Viktor Jansson, was a celebrated sculptor. Jansson herself became well known in her thirties for her Moomin tales and illustrations, which eventually made her world-famous. Because she was and is so recognized for her children's literature, her adult fiction, which she began writing in her early fifties (she died in 2001, aged 86), has tended to be much overlooked, but over her last three decades – a sizeable chunk of an artist's life – the eleven books she wrote were all for adults.

The UK re-publication of *The Summer Book* (1971), in 2003, followed by a selection of her short stories, *A*

Winter Book, in 2006, and the first publication in English of her final novel, *Fair Play*, in 2007, has been revelatory for her English-speaking readership. That there can still be as-yet-untranslated fiction by Jansson is simultaneously an unbelievable aberration and a sheer delight, like a finding of buried treasure every time we're lucky enough to be able to read, for the first time in English, another of her books – especially when the translator is as well suited to her minimal, deeply resonant style as Thomas Teal (who was also the original English translator of *The Summer Book* in the 1970s).

The True Deceiver is another fortuitous first, then, and it is an unassuming, unexpected, powerful piece of work. If the Moomins are Jansson's most celebrated legacy – a community of big-nosed, inventive, good-natured beings who survive, again and again, the storms and existentialisms of a dark Scandinavian winter through simply being mild, kind, inclusive and philosophical – then what will happen when a real community is put in their place? What will the outcome be when Jansson tackles, naturalistically, the life of a tiny hamlet in a dark winter landscape with all its usual viciousness and vicissitudes? And in a book so close to real local life that the original Swedish publication carried a disclaimer stating it was in no way based on any real place and its characters were in no way based on anybody really alive?

A novel about truth, deception, self-deception and the honest uses of fiction, *The True Deceiver* is almost deadpan in its clarity and seeming simplicity. No surprise, then, that this novel is at heart one of her most mysterious, most subtle works. It was her third novel specifically for adults and was first published in 1982. Her biographer, Boel Westin, records that it was a novel with which she had great difficulty. "Its unsparing view of life," Westin comments, "is in fact one of the characteristics of her adult books." Jansson herself commented on the hard graft of it, how "stubbornly, labouriously" she worked on it. There's no doubting the oppressiveness of the conditions under which her characters have to live and work. "The winds had risen. It pressed snow against the windows with a powerful whispering that had followed the people of the village for a long, long time. Between squalls there was silence."

The novel begins with the disarming simplicity which characterizes the whole book. "It was an ordinary dark winter morning, and snow was still falling." There is a darkness, almost banal, there at the heart of the very first sentence. "No window in the village showed a light" in a book about the dark, about a dark place, where snow is a kind of claustrophobia, where "paths filled with snow as quickly as they were shovelled out," where "people woke up late because there was no longer any morning." No longer any morning – the ordinariness is utterly surreal. By paragraph two the judgementalism of small community life has set in; perhaps this mindset is linked to the unrelenting climate? "It's still snowing and there she goes again," the unnamed narrator comments about Katri, one of the novel's protagonists. Katri and her brother are clearly not liked in the village. He's too "simple" and her eyes are the wrong colour. Worse, the brother and sister aren't properly "local".

The novel's voice is flat, exact, a kind of reportage which shifts, quite seamlessly and suddenly, into Katri's own voice, making it not at all clear who the first narrator is and unsettling all notions of objectivity. By the end of this first chapter we're left with this unsettledness, and with the knowledge that this book, concerned with locality, money, winter, wildness, social unacceptability and power, will also be about whether there's such a thing as objectivity. Objectivity and truth happen to be Katri's obsessions. Her refusal to enter into social nicety, her honesty, her silences and her bluntness, have made the villagers uncomfortable and deeply hostile towards her, but made her peculiarly trusted, given her a great deal of power in the community.

It will also be a book very much about the way you look – and the double-take of what a phrase like "the way you look" means: the way you perceive things as well as the way you are perceived by others. It will be about what friendship is, what trade is, what kindness is, and what true currency is. "They say that money smells, it's not true. It's people that smell." It will be about the natural wildness that recognizes something as basic as human "smell" itself as a kind of currency. "Dogs must have seen through us, they must possess a crushing insight that thousands of years of obedience holds in check...How long can what was once a wild animal deny its wildness?" Katri, furred with snow like her dog, counts herself in with the underclass of dogs – will this also be a book about class and hierarchy? At the end of the chapter Katri is standing looking at the local big house, which surreally resembles a giant rabbit's face, and is owned by the artist, Anna Aemelin, who lives there "all by herself, alone with her money". Her motives are clear to her and unhidden from us. She and Mats, her brother, are going to move into that house.

All this, in five short pages. The book begins on the projected standoff, dog versus rabbit – "the real story of Anna and Katri," in other words, the standoff of 'real' versus 'story'. At its heart is a battle that promises to be savage. "I wish the whole village could be covered and erased and finally be clean." Katri wants an obliterating purity; she is a personification of wintriness. Her opponent, Anna Aemelin, has no foothold on winter and is a being particularly associated with spring. "It was winter, and she never worked until the first bare earth began to show." Her art is dependent on the spring, and it almost feels, sometimes, as though the spring might be dependent upon her art. She's also a person practically disconnected from the village, an ageing child living in a veritable museum to her parents, and a famous artist, who draws forest floor pictures known the world over for their authenticity, then takes these "implacably naturalistic" pictures and adds lots of very unnaturalistic flowery rabbits, for which she is equally world-renowned, especially among small children.

Who is the true deceiver here? And how does deception relate to truth? The novel, with its village full of mundane cheats and charlatans, is a philosophical face-off between two mindsets, between Katri's cynicism and Anna's aesthetic sensibility. Is there such a thing as kindness? Or is there only "the whole sloppy, disgusting machinery that people engage in with impunity all the time everywhere to help them get what they want; maybe an advantage, or not even that, mostly just because it's the way it's done, being as agreeable as possible and getting off the hook." What are flowery rabbits (or, it might be added, Moomins) actually for?

Or is it Anna who's right, that the paying of attention to people's needs, though "a pretty rare thing", is a natural and uncynical part of being human? She knows what is expected of her, and she acts on it, just like she knows her own lie and finds it tiresome. But "things are not always that simple". Katri, on the other hand, knows exactly what "simple" means. She has seen and destroyed the snow figures the village children have made in spiteful likeness of her and her too "simple" brother. She knows even more sharply that representation of reality is a loaded concept, for everybody, never mind just for any artist.

"Mats has no secrets. That's why he's so mysterious." Jansson's own texts, works which seem so simple as to be near-throwaway, are always honed to perfection, given a lightness that proves deceptive, an ease of surface which, like a covering of ice over a lake, allows you a rare access to something a lot more risky and profound. "Rarely do books give as clear an impression as yours that they simply matured to the point of inevitability," Jansson's editor at Bonniers, her Swedish publisher, wrote to her when she was struggling with difficult work; in many ways *The True Deceiver* is a book about artistic maturation as well as human coming of age. Like all her fiction, it is a modulation between frozen states and more fluid springlike states. A discussion of the workings of fiction is subtly built in as part of its foundation, with Katri as its fairy-tale villain, or Big Bad Wolf, and with the parallel presence of the simplistic children's stories which Mats and Anna both love, stories of naive world exploration. But this is no fairy tale. Katri's real and secret quest is an unselfish one in a mundane selfish world – to give Mats a secure home and at the same time have the boat that he's designed be made, be brought to exist in the real world. This real boat, a real seagoing possibility, is all the more hopeful and reconciliatory as a symbol here.

Is this an autobiographical portrait? Jansson herself said, quite frankly, at the time of *The True Deceiver*'s first publication in Swedish, that "every serious book is a kind of self-portrait". This overexcited reviewers, who decided to see the book, a subtle and calibrated work, in terms as simplifying and reductive as autobiographical terms almost always are. But the hopelessly innocent Anna Aemelin, totally at a loss with the commercial spinoffs from her flowery rabbits and desperately in need of someone to discipline her administrative habits, is laughably far from the sharp-eyed and wise Jansson who could write so acridly and merrily (as she did in her short story, 'Messages') about the flurry of insane requests that came in from companies and individuals concerning her "product" (asking, for example, for her attention to "Moomin motifs on toilet paper in pastel shades" or "panholders with Moomin figures which I design myself and make in the kitchen without any paid help").

Jansson knew the terrible responsibility and surreality of her position, a position which could result in a request like the one from a company who wanted to use her tiny anarchist figure, Little My, on "a discreet new mini sanitary towel" (she said a discreet no) directly alongside one from a reader asking for a drawing of Snufkin "that I can have tattooed on my arm as a symbol of freedom". She knows that the responsibilities of the artist are huge, the position of the artist surreally powerful. She also suggests that, like Katri, who chooses and edits her words as carefully as any writer, everybody is a kind of artist, with similar responsibilities and comparable powers.

Westin notes in her biography how Jansson often writes herself into her fiction, "sometimes unconcealed, freely, openly, sometimes hidden behind various names and disguises...traces of Tove Jansson run hither and thither in all her texts and pictures, and the patterns they form are constantly new." The key phrase here is constantly new. In *The True Deceiver* both deceivers learn to reinvent themselves.

This novel about art and comfort, about art's place in the dark, is very much about the fact that words mean. It functions like an x-ray through all platitude. It is a deeply poetic work and its images, like the dog which finally runs mad, or the pile of rubbish left on the surface of the frozen lake, all the piled-up ephemera of Anna

Aemelin's life which will sink when the ice melts and the spring comes, are pervasive. On the surface, this is very much a book about how to survive, as well as to deal with what surfaces, in lives, over time. Surely one of its most haunting moments, a moment in which Jansson deals directly with art's impetus, is when Anna, looking through reams and reams of her parents' old correspondence, trying to find a portrait of herself, the artist, as a young girl, discovers that she was hardly there, that "she didn't exist". This is when she realizes, paradoxically, that she became "a painter of the ground" only after both her parents were dead and buried in it.

The True Deceiver is the opposite of charming – and deliberately so. But this novel's presentation of itself as a tough and unresolving work is what might be called a kind of deception in itself. "The struggle between the wild animal...and the rabbit has no real conclusion," Boel Westin writes. "There are no real answers to what is right and what is wrong."

That's one possible reading of the novel. But look at its deep-layered understanding of human surrealities and sadnesses, and at Jansson's usual vision of the epic qualities inherent in all small things. Though meticulous in its rejection of sentimentality, it demonstrates, alongside all the local cruelties, a wealth of small, real kindnesses. More: by the end, its two fixed protagonists, Anna and Katri – the two opposite poles of its "real story" – have actually learned to shift position.

This change doesn't come without fracture – ice

will break in the melt. All the same, at the end of this nimble, mysterious novel, both women have changed their old tunes for new. It is one of Jansson's most deceptively quiet, most astonishing compositions.

—ALI SMITH

THE TRUE DECEIVER

For Maya

1

IT WAS AN ORDINARY DARK WINTER MORNING, and snow was still falling. No window in the village showed a light. Katri screened the lamp so she wouldn't wake her brother while she made coffee and put the Thermos beside his bed. The room was very cold. The big dog lay by the door and looked at her with his nose between his paws, waiting for her to take him out.

It had been snowing along the coast for a month. As far back as anyone could remember, there hadn't been this much snow, this steady snow piling up against doors and windows and weighing down roofs and never stopping even for an hour. Paths filled with snow as quickly as they were shovelled out. The cold made work in the boat sheds impossible. People woke up late because there was no longer any morning. The village lay soundless under untouched snow until the children were let out and dug tunnels and caves and shrieked and were left to themselves. They were forbidden to throw snowballs at Katri Kling's window but did it anyway. She lived in the attic over the storekeeper's shop with her brother Mats and her big dog that had no name. Before dawn she would go out with the dog and walk down the village street towards the lighthouse on the point. She did this every morning, and people starting to get up would say, It's still snowing and there she goes again with her dog and she's wearing her wolfskin collar. It's unnatural not giving your dog a name; all dogs should have names.

People said of Katri that she didn't care about anything except numbers and her brother. And they wondered where she'd got her yellow eyes. Mats's eyes were as blue as their mother's had been, and no one could really remember what their father looked like, it was so long ago he'd gone off north to buy a load of timber and never come back – he'd not been a local man. People were used to the fact that everyone's eyes were more or less blue, but Katri's eyes were nearly as yellow as her dog's. She looked at the world around her through eyes narrowed to slits, so people seldom discovered their unnatural colour, more yellow than grey. But her perpetual distrust, so easily roused, could cause her eyes to open in a sudden straight stare, and in a certain light they were actually yellow and made people very uneasy. People sensed that Katri Kling did not trust or care about anyone except herself and the brother she had raised and protected since he was six years old. That kept people at a distance, that and the fact that no one had ever seen the nameless dog wag its tail. And the fact that the Kling woman and her dog accepted friendliness from no one.

After her mother died, Katri took over helping in the shop, where she also did the accounts. She was very clever. But in October she quit. It was thought that the store-keeper wanted her out of the building but didn't dare say so. The boy Mats didn't count. He was fifteen, ten years younger than his sister, tall and strong and considered a bit simple. He did odd jobs in the village but mostly hung out in the Liljeberg brothers' boat shed when work hadn't stopped because of the cold. The Liljebergs gave him small jobs that were not too important.

There hadn't been any fishing in Västerby for a long time. It didn't pay. There were three sheds that built boats, and one of them took in boats on slips for winter storage and overhaul. The best builders were the Liljeberg brothers. There were four of them, all unmarried. The eldest was Edvard, who designed the boats. In between he drove the mail truck to the market town where he also picked up goods and groceries for the storekeeper. The truck belonged to the storekeeper and was the only vehicle in the village.

The boat builders in Västerby were proud men. They signed every boat with a W, as if the village name were still the venerable Wästerby of olden days. The women crocheted coverlets in old, reliable patterns, and they too signed them with a W, and in June the summer people arrived, bought boats as well as bedspreads, and lived their easy summer life for as long as the warm weather held. Towards the end of August everything went quiet again, back to normal. And by and by came winter.

Now the morning twilight had turned dark blue, the snow had begun to glow, and people had turned on the lights in their kitchens and let their youngsters out. The first snowballs struck the window, but Mats slept peacefully on.

I, Katri Kling, often lie awake at night, thinking. As night thoughts go, mine are no doubt unusually practical. Mostly I think about money, lots of money, getting it quickly and taking it wisely and honestly, so much money that I won't need to think about money any more. And I'll repay it, later. First of all, Mats will get his boat, a big, seaworthy boat with a cabin and an inboard motor, the best boat ever built in this otherwise miserable village. Every night I hear the snow against the window, the soft whisper of the snow blown in from the sea, and it's good, I wish the whole village could be covered and erased and finally be clean... Nothing can be as peaceful and endless as a long winter darkness, going on and on, like living in a tunnel where the dark sometimes deepens into night and sometimes eases to twilight, you're screened from everything, protected, even more alone than usual. You wait and hide like a tree. They say that money smells; it's not true. Money is as pure as numbers. It's people that smell, every one of them with their own furtive stink, and it gets stronger when they're angry or ashamed or when they're afraid. The dog smells it, he knows immediately. If I was a dog, I'd know too much. Only Mats has no smell, he's as clean as snow. My dog is big and beautiful and he obeys. He doesn't like me. We respect each other. I respect the mystery of dogs, the secret natural wildness that big dogs hold on to, but I don't trust them. How can anyone trust big watchful dogs? People give their animals almost human qualities, and they mean noble and attractive qualities. Dogs are mute and obedient, but they have watched us and know us and can smell how pitiful we are. It should astonish us, move us, overwhelm us that our dogs continue, incredibly, to follow us and obey us. Maybe they despise us. Maybe they forgive us. Or maybe they like having no responsibility. We'll never know. Maybe they see us as some sort of unfortunate race of overgrown, misshapen beings, like huge sluggish beetles. Not gods. Dogs must have seen through us, they must possess a crushing insight that thousands of years of obedience holds in check. Why aren't people afraid of their dogs? How long can what was once a wild animal deny its wildness? People idealise their animals, and at the same time they patronisingly overlook a dog's natural life – biting fleas, burying rotten bones, rolling in garbage, barking up an empty tree all night... But what do they do themselves? Bury stuff that will rot in secret and then dig it up and bury it again and rant and rave under empty trees. And the stuff they roll around in! No. My dog and I despise them. We're hidden in our own secret life, concealed in our innermost wildness...

The dog was on its feet, waiting at the door. They went down the stairs and through the shop. In the hall, Katri put on her boots, and all the time her brain kept grinding out threatening night thoughts without any prompting from anywhere. When she came out in the cold and stood still, breathing winter's cleanness, she looked like a tall black monument with the unreachable dog tight by her side as if they'd grown into one. He never wore a lead.

The children went quiet and trudged off through the snow. Around the corner of the first house, they started shrieking again and began to fight. Katri walked on towards the lighthouse. Liljeberg had driven some gas cannisters out to the lighthouse only yesterday, but the tracks had nearly filled with snow. Closer to the point, the northwest wind blew straight in from the sea, and there was the side road leading up the hill to old Miss Aemelin's house. Katri stopped, and the dog stopped instantly as well. On the wind side, both of them were white with snow melting slowly in their fur.

Katri studied the house the way she'd done for some time, every morning on her way towards the lighthouse. In that house Anna Aemelin lived alone, all by herself, alone with her money. Through the whole long winter she almost never appeared, the shop sent what she needed, and Fru Sundblom came once a week to clean. But early each spring, Anna Aemelin's pale overcoat could be seen at the edge of the woods as she moved slowly among the trees. Her parents had lived long lives and never allowed anyone to cut trees in their woods. They'd been rich as trolls when they died. And the woods were still untouch-able. Little by little they had grown almost impenetrable and stood like a wall behind the house; the "rabbit house", they called it in the village. It was a grey wood villa with elabourate carved window frames in white, as grey-white as the tall backdrop of snow-drenched forest. The building actually resembled a large, crouched rabbit – the square front teeth of the white veranda curtains, the silly bay windows under eyebrows of snow, the vigilant ears of the chimneys. All the windows were dark. The path up the hill had not been shovelled.

That's where she lives. Mats and I will live there too. But I have to wait. I need to think carefully before I give this Anna Aemelin an important place in my life.

2

PERHAPS THE REASON PEOPLE called Anna Aemelin nice was because nothing had ever forced her to exhibit malice, and because she had an uncommon ability to forget unpleasant things. She just shook them off and continued on her own vague but stubborn way. In fact, her spoiled benevolence was frightening, but no one had ever had time to notice. On those rare occasions when visitors came to the rabbit house, she dispatched them quickly with an absent-minded graciousness that left them feeling they had paid their respects to some kind of lesser monument. It was not that Anna protected herself with an attitude, nor could it rightly be said that she hid her true face. It was simply that she was only fully alive when she devoted herself to her singular ability to draw, and when she drew she was naturally always alone.

Anna Aemelin had the great, persuasive power of monomania, of being able to see and embrace a single idea, of being interested in one thing only. And that one thing was the woods, the forest floor. Anna Aemelin could render the ground in a forest so faithfully and in such minute detail that she missed not the tiniest needle. Her watercolours were small and implacably naturalistic, and they were as pretty as the springy blanket of mosses and delicate plants that a person walks across in a dense forest but seldom really observes. Anna Aemelin made people see. They saw and recalled the essence of the forest, and, for a moment, experienced a vague yearning that felt pleasant and hopeful. It was a shame that Anna spoiled her pictures by putting rabbits in them, that is to say, Mama, Papa and Baby Bunny. Moreover, the fact that she drew little flowers on the rabbits dispelled much of the deep-forest mystique.

The children's book page had criticised the rabbits on a couple of occasions, and that hurt Anna and shook her confidence, but what could she do? The rabbits had to be there for the sake of the children and the publisher. A new little book came out about every other year. The publisher wrote the text. Sometimes Anna wanted to draw just the ground, the low vegetation, the tree roots – more and more precisely and in a smaller and smaller scale, so deep and close to the moss that its miniature brown and green world became an enormous jungle populated by insects. She could imagine a family of ants instead of rabbits, but now of course it was too late. Anna tidied away her mental picture of the empty, liberated landscape. It was winter, and she never worked until the first bare earth began to show. While she waited, she wrote letters to very small children who wanted to know how the bunnies got flowery fur.

But on the day when the real story of Anna and Katri begins, Anna wrote no letters. She sat in her parlour reading *Jimmy's Adventures in Africa*, a highly entertaining book. He'd been in Alaska the last time.

Anna's long, wide rooms were lovely in the snowlight – the blue-and-white tile ovens, the bright furniture that stood sparsely along the walls and was reflected in the parquet floors that Fru Sundblom polished once a week. Papa had always wanted space around him, he'd been a very big man. And he'd liked blue, a cautious blue colour that was all through the house and that grew paler and paler with the years. A deep serenity lay over the whole rabbit house, an atmosphere of finality.

Later, Anna set aside her book and decided that she ought to call the shop, a thing she disliked doing. The line was busy, so she sat down by the veranda window to wait. Outside on the summer veranda was a large snowdrift that the northwest wind had swept up in a bold curve, both playful and austere. A light, transparent fan of snow whirled above the knife edge at the ridge. This drift described the same line every winter, and it was always equally beautiful. But the drift was too big and too simple for Anna to have noticed it. She called again and the storekeeper answered. Had Liljeberg come back? She had forgotten to mention butter and pea soup; not the big one, a small tin. The storekeeper couldn't hear what she said. He explained that the road still hadn't been ploughed so the mail truck couldn't get through, but that Liljeberg had skied to town and was going to bring the mail and some fresh liver...

"I can't hear!" shouted Anna Aemelin. "Living? Has something happened?"

"Liver," the storekeeper repeated. "There's some fresh liver coming in with Liljeberg and I'll put some aside specially for you, Miss Aemelin, a fine piece of liver..." And then he vanished in the snowstorm; another problem on the line. Anna drew the curtain on the world outside and went back to her book, relieved. Actually, she didn't much care for pea soup. Or for mail.

When Edvard Liljeberg came back from town, he took off his skis and dropped his backpack on the shop steps. His back hurt, and he wasn't in a mood to chat with anyone. He dumped the storekeeper's supplies in a cardboard box and carried them, still wet with snow, into the shop.

"That took time," the shopkeeper said. He was lounging behind the counter, still in a bad temper at losing his shop assistant. Liljeberg didn't answer but went back to the table in the enclosed porch to sort the mail. Katri Kling had seen him from her window as he skied up to the building, and now all at once she was on the porch looking over his shoulder, cigarette in her mouth as usual, examining the mail through the smoke. "That's Miss Aemelin's mail," she said. It was easy to recognise. Most of her letters were decorated with flowers, and the addresses were handwritten by very small children. Katri went on, "Were you going to take it up to her straight away?"

"Can't a man catch his breath?" Liljeberg said. "Being the postman in this village isn't always such a picnic."

She could easily have remarked on the heavy skiing weather, or asked how he could even see the road, or

complained about the town not getting its ploughs out
– anything at all to show interest or pretend to show
interest, the way people talk to make things a little
more pleasant – but no, not Katri Kling. There she stood
squinting through her cigarette smoke, her black hair
like a mane shrouding her face as she leaned over the
table. She had wrapped herself in a blanket against the
cold and held it closed with both hands clenched. She
looks like a witch, thought Edvard Liljeberg.

"I can take the mail up to Miss Aemelin," she said.

"I can't let you do that; it's the postman's job to deliver
the mail. It's a position of trust."

Katri lifted her face and opened her eyes at him;
in the hard light on the porch they were truly yellow.
"Trust," she said. "Don't you trust me?" She paused and
then repeated, "I can take the mail up to Miss Aemelin.
It's important to me."

"Are you trying to help?"

"You know I'm not," Katri said. "I'm doing it entirely
for my own sake. Do you trust me or don't you?"

Afterwards Liljeberg thought that she might anyway
have said that, since she was going out that way with the
dog in any case, it would be no trouble. But at least Katri
Kling was honest – he had to admit that.

* * *

Anna called again. "I can hear you better now," the
storekeeper said. "A small tin of pea soup, you said, and
butter. Liljeberg has come with the mail, and he brought

the liver. It's fresh, straight from the belly, so to speak! I've set some aside for you specially, Miss, but it won't be Liljeberg who brings it this time, but Miss Kling. She's headed out your way."

"Who?"

"My old shop assistant, Katri Kling. She's bringing your liver, she's on her way."

"But liver," Anna objected, but she was just too tired. "Liver is so awful-looking and so hard to prepare... But if you were kind enough to set some aside... This Miss... Kling, you said? Does she know to use the kitchen door?"

And then the line began howling again the way it always did in winter. Anna stood and listened for a while, then she went out to the kitchen and put on some coffee.

Mats came home from the boatyard as dusk came on. In winter, the men in Västerby worked only in mild weather to save on fuel, and the boat shed closed before dark to save electricity. They were very thrifty. Mats was always the last to leave.

"So they got you to leave," the storekeeper said. "I'll bet you'd sit and sandpaper in the dark if they'd let you."

"It's planking now," Mats answered. "Can I have a Coca-Cola on our tab?"

"Yes, sir, right away! Such a shame that your dear sister doesn't want to wait on you any more. Really too bad; she was so quick in the shop. So, planking. You don't say. So you do planking too. Who would have thought?"

Mats nodded without listening and drank his Coca-Cola at the counter, slowly. In the small, overcrowded room, he seemed very large and tall. And his hair was long, much too long, and jet-black like his sister's. Not local hair. He seemed to have forgotten that he wasn't alone. But when Katri came down the stairs, he turned around and the siblings exchanged an imperceptible nod, a little signal of solidarity that was theirs alone. The dog lay down by the door to wait.

The storekeeper said, "So I hear you're delivering the mail to the rabbit villa. Here's the groceries. Watch the liver so it doesn't drip."

"She doesn't like liver," Katri said. "As you well know. She gave that blood pudding to Fru Sundblom."

"Liver isn't blood pudding. Anyway, she ordered it. And remember to go in by the kitchen. Miss Aemelin is particular about her visitors."

This exchange was quiet and hostile, like two wary animals circling for attack.

He doesn't forget, this little storekeeper, he hasn't forgiven me that time. His lust was ludicrous, and I let him know it. I wasn't objective. Things get out of hand every time I lose my objectivity. I have to get away from here.

* * *

The snow was very blue in the early twilight. Katri motioned the dog to wait at the turnoff and walked on up the hill with the wind at her back. No one had shovelled.

Anna Aemelin opened the kitchen door and said, "Miss Kling, how kind of you. And in this weather, there was really no need…"

The woman who entered the house was tall, dressed in some kind of shaggy fur coat, and she didn't smile when she said hello.

It smells of insecurity. This house has been quiet for a very long time. She looks like I thought she would – like a rabbit.

Anna repeated, "Yes, it was nice of you… I mean, it's important to get my mail, but nevertheless…" Anna paused a moment for a reply and then went on. "I've made some coffee. You do drink coffee, don't you?"

"No," said Katri pleasantly. "I don't drink coffee."

Anna was taken aback, more astonished than hurt. Everyone drinks coffee if it's offered. It's only proper; you do it for the hostess's sake. She said, "Tea, perhaps?"

"No thank you," said Katri Kling.

"Miss Kling," said Anna abruptly, "you can put your boots by the door. Water will damage the rugs."

Now I like her better. Let her be an opponent, let me struggle against resistance, amen.

They went into the parlour.

I should have got one of her books. No, I shouldn't, that would have been dishonest.

"Sometimes," said Anna Aemelin, "sometimes I think it might be nice to have a wall-to-wall carpet in here. Something light and very soft. Don't you agree, Miss Kling?"

"No. That would be a shame on such a pretty floor."

Naturally she wants a fluffy floor. Carpet or no carpet, it's all fluffy in here anyway – hot and hairy. Maybe there's more air upstairs. We'll have to crack the windows at night or Mats won't be able to sleep.

Anna Aemelin had her glasses on a thin chain around her neck and now she lifted them, breathed on the lenses and started rubbing them with a corner of the tablecloth. They were probably covered with fluff.

"Miss Aemelin, have you ever had rabbits?"

"Excuse me?"

"Have you had rabbits?"

"No. How do you mean..? The Liljebergs keep rabbits, but I understand they're very troublesome animals..." Anna answered automatically in her own vague manner, her tone of voice never ending a sentence. Then she made a move towards the coffee pot and remembered – this guest didn't drink coffee. Suddenly, sharply, she asked, "And why, Miss Kling, why would I have rabbits? Do you have rabbits?"

"No, I have a dog. A German shepherd."

A dog? Anna's attention began to wander in a different direction. You never knew about dogs...

The untouched coffee service troubled the hostess. She rose and remarked that they needed more light. It was already growing dark, and she lit one softly shaded lamp after another, then suggested that Katri take home an autograph. Anna had beautiful handwriting. When she finished signing her name, she began as usual to draw a rabbit, ears first, stopped herself, and took a fresh sheet of paper. Katri had gone out to the kitchen and put the mail on the kitchen table and the groceries on the counter. Pink juice ran from the package of liver.

"How horrid," said Anna behind her. "Is it blood? I can't stand the sight of blood..."

"Leave it. I'll put it away."

But Anna had opened the package and the liver lay there exposed, brownish red, swollen with blood, small white seams running through the meat. She went pale.

"Miss Aemelin, I'll give it to my dog. I'll take it away. I'm going now."

Quickly, Anna began to explain. She had always been so fearful that things might begin to smell. You put them away and forget them and they start to smell and you start worrying that they'll go bad and have to be thrown out... "And you can't throw out food, the way the world is today..."

"I understand," said Katri. "You hide things, and then they start to smell. Why don't you stop buying things that can start to smell? If you loathe organ meats, then say so. Why do you order liver?"

"It wasn't me, it was him! He was nice enough to put some aside..."

"The storekeeper," said Katri slowly, "the storekeeper – remember this – is not a nice man. He is a very malicious person. He knows you're afraid of liver."

Outside in the back yard, Katri lit a cigarette. Darkness was coming on quickly.

Anna Aemelin hurried to the veranda window and watched her guest go down the hill, a tall dark shape, and down on the road there were two silhouettes, as if a big wolf had come out of the twilight to join her. Side by side they walked back towards the village. Anna stayed at the window in irresolute anxiety. Maybe a cup of coffee would be nice... but suddenly she didn't want one. It was a small but definite insight. She didn't like coffee. In fact, she never had.

3

When Katri got home, she sat down on the bed with her coat on. She was very tired. What had been won? How much had been lost? The first meeting was so terribly important. Katri closed her eyes and tried to get a clear picture of what had happened, but she couldn't manage it. The picture kept slipping away, as soft and diffuse as Anna Aemelin herself, and her shaded lamps and impersonal, well-tuned room and the tentative way they had spoken to one another. But the liver on the kitchen counter, that was tangible, a reality. Did I take it with me for her sake? No. Was it for my own sake, to win points? No, no, I don't think so. It was a purely practical act; there was this bloody thing that frightened her, and it had to go. I wasn't being underhand or dishonest. But you never know, you can never really be sure, never completely certain that you haven't tried to ingratiate yourself in some hateful way – flattery, empty adjectives, the whole sloppy, disgusting machinery that people engage in with impunity all the time everywhere to help them get what they want; maybe an advantage, or not even that, mostly just because it's the way it's done, being as agreeable as possible and getting off the hook... No, I don't think I made myself especially agreeable. I lost this opportunity. But at least I played an honourable game.

Mats had done some new drawings. They were laid out on the table as usual. He never talked about his boat designs, but he wanted Katri to see them. The drawings were always on the same blue-squared paper that made it easier to work out the scale, and the boat was the same: quite large, with an inboard motor and a cabin. Katri noticed that he had altered the curve of the hull. And the cabin was lower. She went carefully through his notes – cost of lumber, motor, labour – facts she would need to check to make sure he wasn't cheated. The drawings were beautifully done. And they weren't just boyish dreams of a boat; they were competent work. Katri knew that they represented long and patient observation, the love and care a person devotes to a single thing, a single overarching idea.

Katri had borrowed books for Mats in town, everything the library had on boats and boat construction and stories of great adventures at sea, mostly boys' books. And at the same time, almost apologetically, Katri had tried to get him to read what she called literature.

"I read them, I do," Mats said, "but I don't get anything out of them. Nothing much happens. I understand they're very good, but they just make me sad. They're almost always about people with problems."

"But your seamen, your shipwrecked seamen? Don't they have problems?"

Mats shook his head and smiled. "That's different," he explained. "And anyway, they don't talk about it so much."

But Katri went on. If Mats got to read four of his own books, then he had to read one of hers, just one. She worried that her brother would lose himself in a world where the bad parts of life were hidden away behind falsely foursquare adventures. Mats read Katri's books to make her happy, but he didn't talk about them. In the beginning, she would ask, and he would say only, "Yes, that was extremely fine." So she stopped asking.

They rarely talked to each other. They owned a silence together that was peaceful and straightforward.

It had been dark for some time when Mats came home. He had probably been with the Liljebergs. Katri didn't like that. He was always hanging around the Liljebergs, hoping they would talk about boats. They were nice to Mats the way people are nice to a house pet. They let him hang around, but he didn't count. Her brother didn't count. Katri put out the food and they ate as usual, each with a book.

These reading meals had always been the most tranquil moment of the day, a complete and blessed peace. But this evening, Katri couldn't read. Again and again, she returned to Anna Aemelin's house, and again and again she left it in defeat. She had ruined everything for Mats. Katri raised her eyes from her book, which she no longer understood, and looked at her brother. The lamp between them had a broken shade and the light fell on his face in a gentle network of light and shadow that made her think of the dappled shadow of leaves under trees or the sun reflecting on a sand bottom. No one but Katri could see how beautiful he was. All at once she had an overwhelming desire to speak to her brother about the implacable goal that never left her thoughts: to explain her notion of honour, defend herself, no, not defend, just explain, just talk to him about everything it was unthinkable to talk about to anyone but Mats.

But I can't. Mats has no secrets. That's why he's so mysterious. No one must ever disturb him; we have to leave him undisturbed in his clean, simplified world. And maybe he wouldn't understand but just worry that I've got problems. And what would I actually explain..? But I know what I have to do. I just have to take what I take completely openly and fight as honourably as I can.

Mats looked up from his book. "What is it?" he said.

"Nothing. Is that a good book?"

"It's great," Mats said. "I just got to the sea battle."

4

EVENINGS IN THE VILLAGE WERE VERY QUIET, just the barking of a mongrel dog or two. Everyone was at home having dinner, and there were lights in every window. As usual, it snowed. The roofs had heavy overhangs of snow, the paths tramped into the snow during the day went white again, and the hard-packed banks on either side grew higher and higher. Inside the snow banks were deep, narrow tunnels where the children had dug hideouts for themselves during thaws. And outside stood their snowmen, snowhorses, formless shapes with teeth and eyes of bits of tin and coal. When the next hard freeze came, they poured water over these sculptures so they'd harden to ice.

One day Katri paused before one of these images and saw that it was a likeness of herself. They had found shards of yellowish glass for eyes and given her an old fur cap, and they'd captured her narrow mouth and her stiff, straight bearing. Attached to this woman of snow was a large snow dog. It wasn't well done, but she could see they meant it to be a dog, and a threatening dog at that. And crouched at the hem of her skirt, very small, was a dwarfish figure with a red potholder on its head. Mats usually wore a red wool cap in winter.

Katri kicked the little figure to pieces, and when she got home she threw her brother's cap in the stove and knitted him a new one in blue. Later she retained a single, grimly valued memory of the children's caricature – the paper they had covered with numbers and driven into the snow woman's heart on a wooden stake. It was, after all, a token of respect from the village. The children listened to their parents' talk and knew she was good at maths. They knew her heart was riddled with numbers.

For years, people had come to Katri and asked her to help them with sums they couldn't do themselves. She handled difficult calculations and percentages with complete ease, and the answers fell into place and were always correct. It began while Katri was doing the store-keeper's ordering and paying his bills. It was then she acquired a reputation for being shrewd, penetrating and good with figures – she discovered that several merchants in town were cheating. Later, she found the storekeeper in the village doing the same thing, but no one knew about that. Katri Kling also had an unerring sense for how sums should be justly allocated and for unambiguous solutions to knotty problems requiring a different kind of arithmetic. The villagers began coming to her with their tax declarations or to talk about bills of sale, wills and property lines. There was a lawyer in town, of course, but they had more faith in her, and why throw money away on a lawyer?

"Give them the meadow," Katri said. "You can't do anything with it anyway; it isn't even good pasture. But put in a clause that says it can't be developed, or sooner or later you'll have them living next door. And you don't like them."

Then she told the opposing party that the meadow was worthless, but they could use it for peace of mind by putting up a fence and a 'No Trespassing' sign so they wouldn't constantly have to hear the neighbours' kids. Katri's advice was widely discussed in the village and struck people as correct and very astute. What made it so effective, perhaps, was that she worked on the assumption that every household was naturally hostile towards its neighbours. But people's sessions with Katri were often followed by an odd sense of shame, which was hard to understand, since she was always fair. Take the case of two families who had been looking sideways at each other for years. Katri helped both save face, but she also articulated their hostility and so fixed it in place for all time. She also helped people to see that they'd been cheated. Everyone was highly amused by Katri's decision in the case of Emil from Husholm. He'd contracted severe septicaemia that had cost him a lot of money and kept him from working for quite some time, and Katri said it was a job-related accident and called for workman's compensation. His employer would have to apply to the employment office on his behalf.

"Well, not really," Emil objected. "It didn't happen while I was building a boat. I was just cleaning some cod."

And Katri said, "When will you learn? Work is work. A cod or a crowbar – it's all the same. Your father was a fisherman, wasn't he? And he worked for the fishery, didn't he? How many times did he injure himself at work?"

"Now and then."

"Of course. And he got no compensation. The government cheated him more times than he knew, so this makes it even."

People could cite many examples of Katri Kling's perspicacity. She seemed to make all the pieces fit together. If people doubted her, they could always have their important papers checked by the lawyer in town. But so far he had never questioned Katri's judgement. "What kind of wise old witch do you have out there? Where did she learn all this?"

In the beginning, people wanted to pay Katri for her services, but when that met a frosty reception, they stopped mentioning compensation. It seemed odd that a person who understood so much about other people's difficulties with out-of-the-ordinary situations should have been so unable to deal with the people themselves. Katri's silence made everyone uncomfortable. She responded to matter-of-fact questions, but she didn't talk. And, worst of all, she didn't smile when she met people, didn't encourage them, didn't help, didn't socialise at all.

"But why do you go to her?" said the elderly Madame Nygård. "Yes, she puts your business to rights, but you no longer trust anyone when you come back. You're different. Leave her alone and try to be nice to her brother."

People did sometimes ask about Mats, but not even that made her more agreeable. She just looked past them with her yellow slits of eyes and said, "Fine, thank you." And when they moved on, it was with a sense that they'd been prying, and they felt very small. So people brought her their problems and then slunk away as quickly as they could.

5

THE CONTINUOUS SNOWFALL carried with it an imprecise darkness that was neither dusk nor dawn, and it depressed people. Things that might have been done with pleasure became merely things that needed doing. Edvard Liljeberg had the winter blues. When work was finished in the boat shed, there was nothing else to do but go home, so all four Liljeberg brothers went home and made dinner. Then they listened to the radio, and the evenings were very long. Edvard Liljeberg decided to overhaul the van, which usually cheered him up. And it wouldn't hurt to have the motor in shape when the township finally got around to ploughing.

Years ago, Edvard drove the schoolchildren into town and was paid by the pound, but now the village had its own school for the lower grades, and the older children rented rooms in town. There weren't so many of them nowadays. Nevertheless, the storekeeper was certainly not losing money on the van. The government paid freight for hauling gas cannisters from the village out to the lighthouse as well as for carrying the mail, on top of which they paid for the petrol. All the same, every time the storekeeper counted out Liljeberg's salary, he was careful to point out what a burden it was for him to perform all these community services. Edvard Liljeberg had nevertheless come to regard the van as his own. It was a Volkswagen, green. And the only vehicle in Västerby.

He turned on the light and pulled his cap down over his ears. It was colder inside than it was outdoors. Working on the van was a private thing, it was no one else's business, and now here was the boy again just inside the door, standing and waiting and waiting and staring at Liljeberg and giving him a bad conscience. Were these qualms about the boy or about his sister? What have we done in this village to deserve these two? What sin have we committed that things can't be normal? Liljeberg swung around and said, "Are you here again? You're never going to learn a damn thing about engines!"

"No," said Mats. "I know."

"Have you been over to Nygård's and chopped wood?"

"Yes."

"What do you want? To help?"

Mats didn't answer. It was always the same. The boy would slink into the garage and just hang around in silence, watching, until the hair on the back of Liljeberg's neck began to stand on end and he couldn't concentrate, but he couldn't be mean to the boy and the whole thing was really annoying, so he just said, "This is hard, this part, so I can't talk right now."

Mats Kling nodded and didn't move. He was so like his sister – the same flat face, though his eyes were blue. Somehow the sister was always around, and her brother was behind her. It was unendurable, and it made Edvard Liljeberg very tired. Finally he said, "If you want, you can pick up a little. It's getting hard to move around in here."

The boy began cleaning up, annoyingly slowly. He started methodically in the far corner and worked his way forwards, moving things and sweeping and organising, almost silently but not quite. It was like having a rat behind the wall – rustling and then silence, scraping and shuffling and then silence again – until Liljeberg turned around and shouted, "Forget that! Come here. Stand here where I can see you. Okay, I'm fixing my van. Watch what I do. But you're never going to learn it for real, and I'm not going to explain anything. So don't talk to me."

Mats nodded. By and by, Liljeberg calmed down and forgot his audience and forgave the intrusion and eventually got the motor running properly.

* * *

But usually Mats was down in the boat shed. He worked in helpless slow motion, but there was great care and patience in his slowness. They could give him small jobs with complete confidence that whatever they entrusted to him would get done. Mostly, they forgot he was there. The Liljeberg brothers gave Mats boring jobs like polishing or filling screwheads. And then all of a sudden Mats would vanish without anyone's having noticed when he left. Maybe he'd promised to fix something for a neighbour, or he'd gone to the woods to do nothing at all. You never knew. Mats Kling had no fixed working hours but came and went as he liked, which of course made it impossible to pay him an hourly wage. Now and then, when the spirit moved them, the Liljebergs paid him – but not much. It seemed to them that he saw work mostly as a form of play, and it's hardly necessary to pay someone for playing. From time to time, Mats would be gone for longer periods, and no one knew or cared where he was.

If it got really cold, it didn't make sense to go on working. The shed wasn't insulated, and the stove was barely able to warm it enough to keep their hands from stiffening. They locked it up and went home. But on the seaward side where the boats were launched, the doors had a latch that was easy to open. Mats would go out on the ice with his cod hook and when no one was in sight he'd go into the boat shed. Sometimes he'd go on with his work, usually details so trivial that no one noticed they'd been done. But most times he just sat quietly in the peaceful snowlight. He never felt cold.

6

THE NEXT TIME EDVARD LILJEBERG skied to town and came back with mail and groceries, Katri Kling was there again wanting the mail for Anna Aemelin. She didn't ask, didn't explain; she just wanted it. Like her brother, she just stood and waited until he gave in.

"All right, then," he said. "Take it. But remember, now and in future, that you're to be very careful with everything having to do with money orders. You're not to misplace even the tiniest scrap of paper, and when it's been signed by Miss Aemelin and properly witnessed it's me who withdraws the money. And when it arrives, she's to have every last penny."

"You amaze me," said Katri, and her voice was very cold. "When have I ever been careless with numbers?"

Liljeberg was silent for a moment and then said, "I spoke hastily. I didn't stop to think. The fact is, there isn't anyone else I would trust with this kind of thing." And he added, "One could say a great many things about you, but at least you're honest."

Katri went into the shop and faced the storekeeper's hatred. "I'm delivering the mail to Miss Aemelin. Has she called to order anything I can take along?"

"No. Miss Aemelin eats out of tins and can't cook. But Liljeberg brought some kidneys."

"Eat them yourself," Katri said. "Eat all the kidneys and liver and lungs you like, but stop being unkind to a woman who can't defend herself."

"But I'm not being unkind," he burst out, genuinely hurt. "I sell to the whole village, and no one's ever said I was unkind..."

Katri interrupted. "One packet of spaghetti, one bouillon cube, two pea soups, small, and a kilo of sugar. I'll take it with me. Put it on her account."

The storekeeper said, very softly, "You're the one who's unkind."

Katri moved on down the aisle. "Rice," she said. "The easy kind." And she added, "Don't make a fool of yourself." It was the same kind of indifferent, dismissive remark that had once seared his desire into hatred. She sounded as if she were giving an order to a dog.

When Katri came to the rabbit house for the second time, she had the dog wait in the back yard. Anna Aemelin had seen her coming up the hill and opened the door at once. After the first breathless courtesies she became quiet and self-conscious. Katri took off her boots and took the groceries into the kitchen.

"I didn't bring fresh meat," she said. "Only tins, things that are easy to fix. The mail came this afternoon with Liljeberg."

"How nice," Anna burst out, and her relief had nothing to do with the mail or the tins but only with the fact that this peculiar person had finally said something that could be used for a normal conversation. "How nice... Tins are so convenient, especially if they're small, they don't go bad... Did I already tell you that raw meat makes me nervous? You know, it doesn't keep, it's like house-plants, such a responsibility, don't you think? Either you water them too little or too much, you never know..."

"No, you never know. But it's too warm here. Houseplants don't like heat."

"No, no, that may be," said Anna vaguely. "I don't know why people always expect me to have plants..."

"I understand. Plants, children and dogs."

"Excuse me?"

"That you're supposed to like houseplants, children and dogs. But I don't suppose you do."

Anna looked up, a sharp look, but the broad, calm face before her expressed nothing. She said, a bit stiffly, "Miss Kling, what an odd remark. Shall we go into the parlour? Although you don't care for coffee."

They went into the parlour. The same soft lighting, the same sense of emptiness and changelessness and dreamlike, compulsory slow motion. Anna sat down and was silent.

"Miss Aemelin," said Katri, very rapidly. "You treat me with greater kindness than I deserve." Suddenly, irration-ally, she wanted out of the rabbit house. She put the mail down in front of Anna and mentioned that there was a postal order that needed a signature. Anna lifted her eyeglasses, looked, and said, "I see it's already been witnessed. But who is this? Such an odd name. Has some foreigner moved into the village?"

"No, I made it up. It's quite an unusual name, don't you think?"

"I don't understand," Anna said. "Surely this isn't the normal procedure."

"I did it to save time."

"But there are several of them, every one with the same peculiar name."

Katri smiled, a quick, somewhat frightening smile that flashed forth like a neon light and abruptly vanished. "Miss Aemelin, I'm very good at signatures. People come to me with their papers and sometimes they want me to sign their names for them. If it would amuse you, I can sign your name, as well."

And Katri Kling signed Anna Aemelin's name, copied precisely from the autograph she'd been given.

"Unbelievable," Anna said. "How clever! Can you draw, as well?"

"I don't believe so. I've never tried."

The wind had risen. It pressed snow against the windows with a powerful whispering that had followed the people of the village for a long, long time. Between squalls there was silence.

Katri said, "I'll go now."

When Anna opened the kitchen door, she caught sight of the dog. His fur was covered with snowy stars and he breathed snowy smoke through his open maw. Anna screamed and tried to slam the door.

"He's not dangerous," Katri said. "He's a very well-behaved dog."

"But he's too big! His mouth was open..."

"He's not dangerous. He's just an ordinary shepherd."

The woman and the dog walked down the hill, equally grey and furry. Anna watched them go. She was still quivering from fright, but her agitation was coloured by a touch of excited curiosity. Katri Kling is adventurous, she thought. Not like the others. But who is it she reminds me of, especially when she smiles..? Not one of Anna's acquaintances, the acquaintances she used to have – no, it was a picture, something in a book. And suddenly Anna began laughing to herself. In fact, the smiling Katri in her fur hat reminded her of the Big Bad Wolf.

* * *

A picture book by Anna Aemelin appeared roughly every other year, a very small book for very small children. The publisher supplied the text. Now the publisher had sent a royalty statement and enclosed a couple of old reviews from last year, which had, unfortunately, with apologies and warmest regards, been mislaid. Anna unfolded the clippings and put on her glasses.

> Aemelin amazes us once again with her unpretentious, almost loving treatment of the miniature world that belongs to her alone – the forest floor. Every detail, meticulously rendered, gives us a jolt of recognition and,

simultaneously, of discovery. She teaches us to see, to truly observe. The text is really only a commentary for children who have just barely learned to read, and it does not vary much from one little book to the next. But Miss Aemelin's watercolours are perpetually fresh. Her frog's-eye perspective, naive as well as terribly accomplished, captures the essence of the forest, its silence and its shadow. What we have before us is the untouched primeval forest. Only the tiniest reader will venture to tread on her mosses, with or without rabbits. We are convinced that every child...

Anna always stopped reading when they started on the rabbits. The other clipping had a picture, the usual one that they used far too often. The caricature was good-natured, but the artist was thinking 'rabbit' more than 'Anna'. He had lavished attention on her front teeth, square, with small gaps between, and on the whole she looked fluffy, white and vacant. Now I mustn't be silly, she thought. After all, it's not everyone gets their picture in the paper. But next time I must remember not to show my teeth and to hold up my chin. If only they didn't always insist on a smile...

Anna Aemelin's natty little books with their washable covers are always received with pleasure. They have been translated into several languages. This year's story focuses principally on the gathering of blueberries and lingonberries. With all due respect to Miss Aemelin's convincing and captivating presentation of the Nordic forest, one must nevertheless wonder whether her really rather stereotyped rabbits…

Yes, yes, said Anna to herself. Things are not always that simple – not for me, not for anyone…

The children's letters would have to wait for another time. Safe in her room, Anna drew up the coverlet, turned on the lamp as the daylight began to wane, opened to her bookmark, and read on. And as she read about *Jimmy's Adventures in Africa,* her tranquillity returned, as she had hoped it would.

7

IT GREW COLD IN EARNEST. Again and again Liljeberg had to shovel the path to Miss Aemelin's so that Fru Sundblom, with her bad legs, could get up the hill to clean. She went only once a week, and the upstairs had been shut for years, but it was nevertheless too much for an old woman, and Fru Sundblom often bewailed her fate.

"But you make a good living crocheting coverlets," said Madame Nygård. "Tell Miss Aemelin that the cleaning is too hard for you. There are younger women who can take over. Katri Kling quit her job in the shop, and she carries the mail up to the rabbit house. Mention it to her."

"To her!" Fru Sundblom exclaimed. "You know yourself that you can't just go talk to Katri Kling. At least, I can't. I have my principles."

"For example," said Madame Nygård.

But Fru Sundblom didn't seem to be listening. She looked grimly out of the window, said the usual things about the snow, then very soon went home. When people came to visit Madame Nygård, they were always offered the rocking chair. Only Fru Sundblom was so nervous and so full of annoyance that she couldn't stand to sit and rock. She always sat on the sofa-bed by the door. Perhaps she was the only one who failed to sense how unusually peaceful it was in the big kitchen, despite the different generations going in and out, a peacefulness that put people at ease and made them forget to hurry.

Madame Nygård mostly hovered around the huge cooking stove or sat on her chair by the hearth with her hands folded lightly across her stomach. Everyone else in the village had torn out these stoves because they took up so much space, and now their kitchens were dreary and lacked a heart. But the Nygård kitchen was the way it always had been. And when the daughters and daughters-in-law crocheted, they used her patterns and the colours chosen by her grandmother. The Nygård coverlets sold best. There had once been talk of having a shop in the market town to sell the coverlets, and people turned to Katri Kling as usual for advice. But she said, "No, no middlemen. They take too big a commission. You'll lose money on the deal. Let people come out here, make it hard for them. Make them search for their coverlets, make them hunt."

Katri crocheted like all the others. But she used colours that were too strong – and far too much black.

It snowed on and on and they heard not a word about ploughing, so Liljeberg continued skiing to town although he didn't like it. Because he was a nice man, he took on private commissions, provided they were small – medicine, for example, maybe underwear or indoor plant food, yarn if some woman had run out completely. He didn't have much room in a backpack and a sledge, and he had to give first priority to the mail and fresh food for the storekeeper. People sorted out their orders on the storekeeper's porch. But Liljeberg refused point blank to go to the library. He told Katri she could borrow books for Mats from Miss Aemelin, who had long shelves full of books. He'd seen them.

But Katri didn't want to talk to Anna Aemelin about books. She no longer took off her boots when she brought the mail to the rabbit house; just said hello and an unavoidable word or two and then walked on with her dog. Katri had given up. She understood it was not possible for her to make use of an amiability she didn't possess, the simple friendliness it would have taken to get closer to Anna Aemelin but which lay unattainably beyond the boundaries that Katri, in her self-sufficiency, had drawn.

* * *

Madame Nygård called Anna and asked if she would like to come for coffee. It wasn't at all far, and one of the boys could come to get her.

"How kind," said Anna, who liked Madame Nygård very much. "But it's grown so terribly cold and, you know, it's just such an effort to venture out..."

"Yes, I understand. A person mostly goes out when she has to. Or when she just wants to be outdoors. Let's wait and see. How are you? Is everything going all right?"

"Yes, thank you," said Anna. "Thank you for calling."

Madame Nygård was silent for a moment and then added, "Your father often walked through the village. I remember him so well. He had a very beautiful beard."

Katri brought mail that same day.

"Don't go yet," Anna pleaded. "Not right away. Miss Kling, you've been so helpful. I would very much like to show you Papa's and Mama's home."

They walked through the house together, from room to room, each with its own untouchable tidiness. Katri saw no great difference between the rooms, all of them a faded blue and vaguely depressing. Anna kept up a running explanation. "Here's Papa's chair where he read his newspaper. No one but Papa was allowed to fetch the paper from the shop and he always read them in order, although they arrived so seldom... And here is Mama's evening lamp – she embroidered the shade herself. This photograph was taken in Hangö..."

Katri was very quiet except for an occasional gruff comment, and eventually she was guided up to the second storey where it was bitterly cold. "It's always been cold," Anna explained, "but it was only the maid who lived up here. The guest rooms were almost always empty. Papa didn't really like having guests; they disturbed his routines, you know... But he wrote a great many letters and mailed them himself in the shop... You know, Miss Kling, although Papa knew hardly anyone in the village, they would all take off their caps when he walked by, just spontaneously."

"Did they?" Katri said. "And he tipped his hat?"

"His hat," Anna repeated, puzzled. "If he even had a hat... So odd – I can't remember his hat..." And she went on with her narrative.

Katri could see that Anna was very excited. She talked too much. Now it was about her mother, who went around to the poor people in the village and distributed white bread at Christmas.

"They weren't offended?" Katri said.

Anna looked up, quickly, then away again. She continued bravely on about Papa's stamp album, Mama's recipe book, the dog Teddy's pillow, Papa's almanac in which he made notes on good and bad deeds to be thoroughly reviewed on New Year's Eve. Anna ran amok through her parents' house, revealing everything and thus, for the first time, calling its worth and charm into question. She dashed onwards, unable to stop, possessed by a wicked sense of liberation in shattering taboos, forcing her unwilling guest to see more and more, hear more and more of Papa's anecdotes, little stories whose point was annihilated even before she exposed them to Katri's silence. It was like laughing in church. The inviolable was opened to a great, treacherous attack, and Anna let it happen. Her voice rose and became shrill and she stumbled over thresholds until Katri very tactfully took her arm and said, "Miss Aemelin, I really must go now." Anna became very quiet. Katri added, kindly, "Your parents must have been exceptional individuals."

Out in the yard, Katri lit a cigarette, the dog joined her, and they walked down to the road. Doubt returned, repeating over and over, Why did I say that? For her sake, so she doesn't have to feel she's betrayed her idols? No! For my own sake? No! Somebody goes into a spin and has to be checked, that's all; someone goes too far and has to be stopped.

When Katri had gone, Anna went cold. All of a sudden the whole house seemed full of people. She had an irrational desire to phone someone, anyone at all, but what was there to say? Maybe not much more than that; she'd said far too much... In any case, Anna thought, there's one thing I didn't reveal. I didn't show her my work.

Although that had nothing whatever to do with Mama and Papa.

* * *

On cleaning Wednesday, as Fru Sundblom was on her way home from the rabbit house, she met Katri and her dog on the hill and stopped and said, "Not that it matters in the least, but Miss Aemelin hasn't had any fresh food for weeks, and I was the one who used to fetch it for her."

"Miss Aemelin doesn't like organ meats," Katri answered.

"And how do you know that?"

"She said so."

"And why have you rearranged the refrigerator?"

"It was dirty."

Fru Sundblom went slowly red in the face, and she seemed to swell and fill the road as she replied. "Miss Kling, cleaning is my area, and I clean the way I've always cleaned, and I don't like other people sticking their noses in my business."

Katri smiled without answering, the wolf smile that could put anyone off balance, and Fru Sundblom shouted, "Well! I see! I guess I know when certain people are trying to curry favour with the old lady just because she's losing her grip." And the big woman stalked off down the hill.

When Katri came into the rabbit house, she put down her bag in the hall and announced that she couldn't stay.

"Don't you have time? Not even a little while?"

"Yes, I do have time. But I can't stay."

"Miss Kling, wouldn't you like to stay?"

"No," Katri answered.

Then Anna smiled, and without a trace of her usual confusion, she said, "Do you know, Miss Kling, you're a very unusual person. I've never met anyone so terribly – and I use the word in the sense of frightening – so terribly honest. I want you to listen, now, because I think what I have to say is important. You're young, and perhaps you don't yet know so much about life, but believe me, almost everyone tries to play a part, to be what they're not." Anna thought for a moment. "Not Madame Nygård, but that's another matter... You know, I notice much more than people realise. Don't misunderstand me – of course they mean well. I've met nothing but kindness my whole life. Nevertheless... you, Miss Kling, are always yourself, and that feels somehow...", she hesitated, "...different. I trust you."

Katri looked at Anna, who, entirely in passing, in

friendly earnest, had given the go-ahead for an author-ised conquest of the rabbit house.

Anna continued. "Now don't take this the wrong way, Miss Kling, but I find your way of never saying what a person expects you to say, I find it somehow appealing. In you there's no, if you'll pardon my saying so, no trace of what people call politeness... And politeness can sometimes be almost a kind of deceit, can it not? Do you know what I mean?"

"Yes," said Katri. "I do."

* * *

Katri walked on out towards the point with the dog. The snow had a crust hard enough to walk on. Spring was coming, a spring that belonged to Katri Kling, Katri Kling who in open and honourable play had finally won a round, who had everything she wanted to achieve within reach. A new strength coursed through her. She ran straight out on the snowdrifts at the beach, broke through the crust, stopped, up to her knees in snow, raised her arms and laughed. The dog, back on the lighthouse road, growled, a low, warning growl deep in his throat. "Quiet," said Katri. "Heel." She was giving orders to herself. Now it was only a question of self-control and concentration. The game could continue, and now she could fight with her own weapons. Which she believed were pure.

8

"HERE ARE SOME POSTAL ORDERS I've signed and witnessed, but you should have a look at them, Miss Aemelin. And here's the money Liljeberg picked up last time."

"How kind of you," Anna said, shoving the envelope full of money into her desk.

"But aren't you going to count it?"

"Why?"

"To make sure it's right."

"My dear Miss Kling," said Anna, "I am certain that it's right. Is he still skiing into town?"

"Yes, he is." Katri paused for a moment. "Miss Aemelin, there is something I want to speak to you about. Liljeberg overcharged you for shovelling and fixing the drain – both labour and materials. I mentioned it to him and he returned the difference. Here it is."

"But you can't do that," Anna exclaimed. "That just isn't done... And how can you be sure?"

"I checked the going price and asked him how much he'd charged. It was simple."

"I don't believe it," Anna said. "Absolutely not. All the Liljebergs like me, I know they do..."

"Believe me, Miss Aemelin, people like you a little less when they can cheat you."

Anna shook her head. "How awkward," she said. "And just when it's snowing in through the attic window..."

"Believe me," Katri said again. "It's not awkward. Liljeberg will come and fix the window whenever you say, and he'll do it with new respect and at a good price."

But Anna couldn't let it go. She insisted that the whole business was tedious and unnecessary, and that she and Liljeberg could never again treat each other naturally. Moreover, money didn't always matter as much as people seemed to think.

"It may well be that the marks and the pennies are not so important," Katri answered. "What is important is being honest and not cheating, not even on the pennies. The only justification for taking another person's money is if you can make it grow and then give them a fair return."

"My dear, you suddenly have a great deal to say," said Anna, her thoughts elsewhere.

Katri grew careless. Irritated by the conversation, she said, "While we're on the subject, how much do you pay Fru Sundblom?"

Anna drew herself up and said, very stiffly, in the same tone of voice her father had used when he occasionally spoke to a domestic, "My dear Miss Kling, that is a detail that I really cannot recall."

9

MATS KLING AND LILJEBERG met on the village street.

"So you're out walking the dog," said Liljeberg.

"Yes. I'm going up to visit old Miss Aemelin and talk about her attic window."

"I heard you were going to fix it. It's snowing in, they say."

"And the sink is blocked."

"Right. Your sister is in charge, but it's just as well. Now we've got a thaw, we were thinking we'd get back to work in the boat shed. We've got some little jobs for you. By the way, I've noticed you let yourself in from the water side."

"But you didn't tell the others."

"No, why should I? I see the township's finally ploughed the roads."

Mats nodded.

"And Fru Sundblom is going to stop cleaning for Miss Aemelin," Liljeberg went on. "They say the hill is too steep for her old legs, but some people have other ideas."

Mats nodded again without listening.

They said goodbye and continued their separate ways.

The fir trees stood so close to the rabbit house that the back yard was always in shadow. It's lonely here, Mats thought. It's a very lonely house, maybe because it's so big. The dog lay down in his usual place by the kitchen steps with his nose between his paws.

"So this is Mats," said Anna Aemelin. "It was nice of you to come. And you brought your tools, I see. But the window isn't so urgent... Take off your boots and come in for a bit." She looked at the dog. "Why can't he come in and get warm? Your sister never lets him come in."

Mats answered that the dog was probably better off outdoors.

"But maybe he's thirsty. Or does he eat snow?"

"I don't think so."

"Nice dog," Anna called to him. "What's his name?"

"Please don't worry about him. He's fine." Mats took off his boots.

They had coffee in the parlour. Mats did not try to talk to his hostess, but he smiled at her occasionally and looked around with an appreciation that pleased her.

"It's the snowlight," she said. "Everything's pretty in snowlight." Anna liked Mats Kling. The moment he came in, she felt comfortable with him. What different temperaments siblings can have. Though neither of them was very talkative.

"You know," said Anna, "in the beginning I was almost a little frightened of your sister. So silly of me."

"Very silly," Mats agreed and smiled again.

"Yes. The same way you can be anxious about a big strange dog, although it just stands perfectly still. Now I'm so glad that Katri has promised to come and help me with the cleaning."

Fru Sundblom's formidable shadow glided past for one angry moment. Anna shook her off and sighed and the room was silent again.

Mats said, "Miss, I see you're reading *Jimmy's Adventures in Africa*. That's a good book."

"It is good."

"Yes. But *Jimmy's Adventures in Australia* is even better."

"You don't say. Is Jack still with him?"

"No. Jack stayed in South America."

"Really," Anna said. "That's too bad. I mean, if two friends begin an adventure they should go on together, or it's just not fair." She stood up. "Come and have a look at my books," she said. "Have you read Forester's sea stories?"

"No."

"And Jack London?"

"Someone had taken it out."

"My dear young friend," Anna cried. "Don't say another word until you've read them. Talk about adventures! You have no idea!"

Mats laughed. Anna's bookcase was a tall, white, ornamental object with carved columns at the corners. Together they went through the shelves, thoroughly, with the short questions and comments people devote to things that really matter. Anna's shelves held nothing but adventure books – on land, at sea, in balloons, down in the bowels of the earth, and on the deepest ocean floor. Most of the books were very old. Anna's father had collected them in the course of a long life that in every other respect had been entirely free of irrational fantasies. Anna sometimes thought that, of all the things her father had taught her to respect, this book collection was the best. But it was a shy thought, and she did not allow it to overshadow his other opinions.

When Mats went home with a bundle of books, there had been no discussion of the attic window. He promised to come back the next day with *Jimmy's Adventures in Australia*. And Anna had a long phone conversation with the bookshop in town.

* * *

Mats fixed the window and the drain. He shovelled snow and chopped wood and lit fires in Anna's pretty tile stoves. But usually he just came to borrow books. A cautious, almost timid friendship began to grow between Anna and Mats. They talked only about their books. In tales where the same heroes returned in book after book, they could refer familiarly to Jack or Tom or Jane, who had recently done this or that, as if gossiping in a friendly way about acquaintances. They criticised and praised and were horrified, and they discussed in detail the happy ending with its just division of the inheritance and its wedding and its villain getting his just deserts.

Anna read her books afresh, and it seemed suddenly as if she had a large circle of friends, all of whom lived more or less adventuresome lives. She was happier. When Mats came in the evenings, they would drink tea in the kitchen while reading their books and talking about them. If Katri came in, they were quiet and waited for her to leave. The back door would close, and Katri would have gone.

"Does your sister read our books?" Anna wanted to know.

"No. She reads literature."

"A remarkable woman," Anna observed. "And on top of that she's got a head for maths."

10

THE FIRST SPRING STORM SWEPT IN FROM THE SEA, a strong warm wind. The snow was already heavy and fragile, and in the stormy forest great clumps of snow fell from the branches, and many branches broke in the moment of their liberation. The whole forest was full of movement. In the evening, Anna walked in under the trees behind the house. She stood for a long time and listened. As always when the landscape readied itself for spring, there was a great unease that Anna recognised and welcomed. As she listened, her rabbit face changed, grew tighter, almost severe. The wind's assault on the trees produced voices, music, distant cries. Anna nodded to herself. The long spring was just beginning.

Soon she could approach the ground.

* * *

The storm continued the following day. Katri came home and stamped off the snow on the steps. The shop was full of people and smelled sour of sweat and tension. In the sudden silence, Fru Sundblom said, "Well, good afternoon? And how is Miss Aemelin today? No new autographs?"

The storekeeper laughed. Katri walked past them towards the stairs.

"Well, like I said," said Emil from Husholm, "these are wicked times and it pays to keep an eye out. They can come here, too; it's not that far. Pretty soon we'll have to start locking our doors at night."

"What did the constable say?" Liljeberg wanted to know.

"What would he say? He goes around and asks questions and then he goes home and writes a report. I heard they even took the damper cord."

"Jesus help us!" Fru Sundblom exclaimed. "And Miss Aemelin, who doesn't have a proper lock on a single door! Well, she's going to have to take care."

Katri stopped on the stairs.

"Didn't he see anything, poor man?" Liljeberg asked.

"Nothing. He heard someone making noise in the house, so he went in, and before he knew it they hit him on the head. That's how they do it."

Mats was lying on his bed reading. "Hi," he said. "Did you hear about the break-in at the ferry slip?"

"I heard," said Katri, hanging up her coat.

"But isn't it exciting?"

"Yes, very," she said. At the table by the window, with her back to Mats, she opened one of his books at random and let the room go quiet. Katri never realised that the book she hid her thoughts behind was called *Karl Outwits the Police*, which was just as well. She wouldn't have seen the humour in it.

As Katri planned her fictitious break-in at the rabbit house, she did not for one moment have a sense that the enterprise was rather childish. She knew only that she had a chance, an opportunity she must exploit before the wind shifted and the excitement in the village died down.

It was late at night when Katri motioned for the dog to follow. She took a torch, her gloves, a potato sack, and went out into the blizzard. The wind howled in over the coast the way it would in a really good adventure story, and she had a hard time finding her way. The torch wasn't much help. Again and again she stumbled into snowdrifts by the side of the road and had to back up. It was slow going. She missed the turnoff road and had to retrace her steps. The dog waited in his usual place outside the kitchen door, but Katri did not take off her boots. On the contrary, she dragged in as much snow as she could across the carpets. Inside, the storm seemed closer, the wind came in gusts, in violent onslaughts like some consciously malignant force. Katri put the torch on the sideboard where the family silver stood in a row – Katri had polished it herself – and in the narrow beam of light she put it all in the potato sack: the coffee pot, the sugar bowl, the cream jug, the samovar, the dessert bowl. Very carefully she pulled out several drawers and emptied them out on the floor. She left the kitchen door open when she left.

It was a very simple break-in. Katri saw it as a purely practical matter without a trace of drama or questionable ethics. She had simply moved a piece on the board game of money, and Anna was nothing more than an opponent confronting a new move.

Down on the road, Katri tossed the potato sack into a snowdrift and went home. For the first time in ages, she slept in a cradle of gentle dreams free of desolation and anxiety.

Anna took the break-in with surprising calm, but the villagers were extremely upset. They didn't know Anna Aemelin, most of them hardly knew what she looked like, since she almost never appeared on the road, but she had become a concept, something of an old landmark that had been in place forever. Laying hands on old Miss Aemelin's rabbit villa was unseemly, almost like vandalising a chapel or a shrine. One neighbour after another came to offer sympathy. Those who had never been inside the rabbit villa made up for it now. The sideboard drawers still lay on the floor in disarray, and no one was permitted to touch them, or anything else, until the constable had been there. Anna explained that there could be fingerprints. The potato sack full of silver stood inside the kitchen door and was also not to be touched. Several of the guests had made coffee cakes and the Liljebergs brought a small bottle of cognac.

Anna got a good deal of pleasure from her meeting with the town constable. She told her story and tried in every way to help him reconstruct the crime. Katri made coffee for everyone, and Anna was given more good advice than she could remember. It was Madame Nygård who summed up the general view: as long as the neighbourhood was unsafe, Anna Aemelin could not live alone. The village simply could not take responsibility for such a thing. Madame Nygård proposed Katri Kling as a temporary protector and added that it would be a good idea to have the dog by the door for a time. Madame Nygård was regarded as very old and experienced; even the constable agreed that she was right. When coffee had been served, he went back to town to write a report and the villagers went about their business and finally only Anna and Katri were left in the parlour.

"Well, well," said Anna, "what a circus this turned out to be. But I can't understand why he didn't take fingerprints. They usually do. And no one can explain why the burglar threw the bag in the ditch. Who could have frightened him..? There's not a soul out at night around here. Maybe a dog? Because it couldn't have been his conscience... Do you think some dog might have been out last night?"

"That's what I think," Katri said.

Anna sat and thought for a while and then suddenly asked if Katri read detective stories.

"No, I don't."

"Neither do we... I sit here thinking about what Madame Nygård said... that it's not hard to be cocky in the morning but it feels different in the twilight. It was nice of you to promise to come with your dog. But only for a couple of nights. Then I'll probably have forgotten the whole thing. I forget so easily..."

11

KATRI MOVED INTO THE RABBIT HOUSE and the dog got his place in the hall by the kitchen door. Katri was in such a state of nerves the first day that the simplest tasks seemed too much for her. She was sure of just one thing: she needed to move very quietly and be as invisible as possible, a shadow in no way encroaching on Anna's long pampered and protected life. And time was short, every hour counted. Katri had only a few days to take possession of the house and convince Anna that independence was possible even if you weren't alone. But Anna just sat by the fire and froze. She felt the cold more than ever and wondered why her house had never before seemed so absolutely empty and forsaken.

Katri came in to say goodnight. "I don't think," she said cautiously, "I don't think the lock matters so much..."

"What?" said Anna, leaping to her feet. "What lock?"

"I mean, there's no decent lock on the door. But if you start shutting yourself in now, then it's one more thing to attend to. I mean, a new worry..."

Anna was irritated. "What are you talking about?" she said. "Why would I shut myself in? This place is shut in enough already! Calm down and go to bed."

* * *

In the morning, an invisible Katri had put a breakfast tray beside Anna's bed. Fires in the tile stoves, a bowl of periwinkles, the hem of her dressing gown mended. The right book opened to the bookmark beside Anna's plate. A lot of small things, everywhere, all day. But Katri continued to be invisible. Anna grew more and more uneasy, it was like having a spirit in the house, one of those magically enslaved and obedient pixies that frequent the castles in fairytales, diligent creatures, ever-present but always just vanishing. You catch a glimpse of movement and turn around – but there's nothing there, a door closing silently.

For the first time in her solitary life, Anna noticed the silence of the house, and it made her flesh crawl. By evening, she was beside herself and went out to the kitchen – making a careful detour around the dog. The kitchen was empty. So she ran up the stairs and shouted outside her door, "Miss Kling! Are you in there, or where in the world are you?"

Katri opened the door. "What is it?" she said. "What's happened..?"

"Nothing," Anna said. "That's just it – nothing. You sneak around and I never know where you are. It's like having mice in the walls!"

* * *

Katri changed her tactics. Her quick steps were heard everywhere, she rattled the dishes, she started beating rugs in the yard, and she came often to seek Anna's advice about this or that. Finally Anna said, "But my dear Miss Kling, why are you asking me about things that you can very well decide without my help? You're no longer yourself. I can assure you that you needn't be nervous, there's no cause for alarm."

"Miss Aemelin, I don't understand."

"The break-in, of course," said Anna impatiently. "Our burglar."

Katri started to laugh. Katri's laugh had nothing in common with her terrifying smile. Her whole face opened in a peal of unalloyed hilarity – with very pretty teeth.

Anna gazed at her attentively and said, "I've never seen you laugh. Do you not often laugh?"

"No, not often."

"And what is it that's so amusing? Our burglary?"

Katri nodded.

"Well, amusing and amusing. All the same, you're no longer yourself, whatever the reason. You were nicer in the beginning."

At three o'clock, the phone rang, and Katri answered.

"Oh, it's you," said the storekeeper. "Miss Aemelin doesn't answer her own phone any more? Tell her the police caught them. They broke into another house. How are the guard duties going?"

Katri said, "Set aside two bottles of milk and some yeast and put it on the bill."

"Are you baking now, too? Sounds like the rabbit house is becoming a real establishment."

"Yes, that's all. I'll call if there's anything else." Katri hung up the receiver and started back to the kitchen.

"But why did the storekeeper call?" Anna asked behind her. "He's never called before."

"I ordered some yeast. You've got flour." Katri stopped in the half-open door, looking straight at Anna. Finally she said, quickly, "They caught them."

"What did you say?"

"The burglars. The danger is past."

"Well, that's good news," Anna said. "It surprises me, I didn't think that constable seemed terribly competent. By the way, before I forget, would you ask Mats to look at the stove in your room? It doesn't draw, it never has. If this weather continues, we'll have you down with a cold or something," she added dismissively and went back to her book.

* * *

Towards evening, Katri brought in wood to light a fire in the parlour. "It's very wet," she said. "There ought to be a roof over the woodpile. A woodshed."

"Can't be done. Papa wouldn't have a woodshed."

"But we're going to get a lot of rain."

"My dear Miss Kling," said Anna, "we've always had the firewood by the side of the house, and a shed would destroy the building's lines."

Katri smiled her grim smile and said, "Well, this house isn't all that beautiful. Although I've seen even worse from the period."

When the wood was finally burning, Anna sat down in front of the stove and said, "It's so nice having a fire." And then, casually, "And so nice that you seem to be getting back to normal."

The next day, Anna declared that she wanted to have a little party for the three of them. Katri was not to eat in the kitchen today. They'd use the silver and have wine and candles.

Anna closely supervised the setting of the table and made certain changes to small detailed arrangements that a person of Katri's generation and background would not have been taught as a matter of course. Mats arrived at the appointed hour, amiable and a little self-conscious. They took their places at the table. Anna had dressed for dinner. The role of hostess had never presented her with any difficulty, but today her social instincts and sensitivity were not what they should have been. After a few unconnected observations that did not lead to conversation, she allowed the meal to proceed without appearing to notice the silence of her guests. Every time Katri stood up to serve, Anna lifted her eyes quickly and then looked away. The table was lovely beneath the crystal chandelier, with all its lamps burning. Even the sconces were lit. The dessert came in.

Anna touched her wineglass but didn't raise it. Her sudden immobility was transferred to her guests, and for one frozen moment the room was as rigid as a photograph.

"Attention," Anna said. "Giving another human being your undivided attention is a pretty rare thing. No, I don't think it happens very often... Figuring out what someone wants and longs for, without being told – that probably requires a great deal of insight and thought. And of course sometimes we hardly know ourselves. Maybe we think it's solitude we need, or maybe just the opposite, being with other people... We don't know, not always..."

Anna stopped talking, searched for words, raised her glass and drank. "This wine is sour. I wonder if it hasn't stood too long. Don't we have an unopened bottle of Madeira in the sideboard somewhere? No, let it go. Don't interrupt me. What I'm trying to say is that there are few people who take the time to understand and listen, to enter into another person's way of living. The other day it occurred to me how remarkable it is that you, Miss Kling, can write my name as if I'd written it myself. It is characteristic of your thoughtfulness, your thoughtfulness for me and no one else. Very unusual."

"It's not especially unusual," Katri said. "Mats, pass the cream. It's simply a matter of observation. You observe certain habits and behaviour patterns, you see what's missing, what's incomplete, and you supply it. It's just a matter of experience. Get things working as best you can, then wait and see."

"Wait and see what?" said Anna. She was annoyed.

"How it goes," Katri said, looking straight at Anna, her eyes at this moment deeply yellow. She continued very slowly. "Miss Aemelin, the things people do for one another mean very little, seen purely as acts. What matters is their motives, where they're headed, what they want."

Anna put down her glass and looked at Mats. He smiled at her. He hadn't been listening.

"Miss Kling," Anna said, "you worry about such peculiar things. If people come up with some pleasant way of helping or making you happy, then it's just exactly what it appears to be... What became of that Madeira? Or port. Whatever you can find. Take Papa's best glasses, they're on the top, on the right. And don't interrupt me, I have something to say." Anna waited impatiently. When the glasses were filled, she declared quickly, almost angrily, that since the upper floor was empty, it would be a purely practical arrangement for Katri and Mats to move in. She forgot to propose a toast, rose from the table, wished them a pleasant evening, further discussion could wait for tomorrow, and would Mats please close the damper when the fire was completely out.

Once in her room, Anna was gripped by alarm. She stood inside the door, trembling violently, waiting, but Katri didn't come. Katri should have come. Finally, Anna crept in under the coverlet and hid from her irrevocable decision – to be alone no more. She was too warm. The silence lasted too long. Anna threw off the covers and jumped out of bed. The parlour was empty. In the hall she tripped over the dog she wasn't used to, mumbled an apology, and was finally out in the snow.

The door banged behind her in the wind. A few steps into the woods and the cold swept over her like a gentle warning. She stopped. Katri stood quietly in the kitchen window, waiting. Anna came back, the door slammed, and for a long moment there was quiet. Then Anna shouted loudly and very angrily, "Miss Kling! Your dog is shedding, there's hair everywhere. You need to comb your dog!"

Katri waited until Anna's steps moved on, then she drew a deep breath and continued washing the dishes in silence.

12

THE MOVE WAS MADE IN LILJEBERG'S VAN and was very simple: a few cardboard boxes, two suitcases, a small table, and a bookcase.

"No problem," said Liljeberg. "It's practically next door. Not every village has its own transport!" It was nice to hear him laugh. Katri had scrubbed the room above the storekeeper's shop, scrubbed it with a kind of painstaking rage, the way women clean when they can't lash out. She scrubbed away the neighbours' shamefaced talk about envy and petty favours, she scrubbed away all the black night thoughts, and most of all she scrubbed the doorway where the storekeeper used to loiter on some pretext, standing in hungry vigilance, waiting for some sign to tell him if he could go on hating or if there was the tiniest little handhold for his lust. The room became as clinically clean and naked as a wave-washed skerry.

Liljeberg loaded the suitcases. "Jump in, little witch," he said. "Cinderella on her way to the castle!" When he started the engine, the storekeeper shouted, "Give my regards to Miss Aemelin! Tell her I'm getting in some rabbit! Fresh, just killed! Just for her..." The village children ran after the van a little way, shrieking and throwing snowballs.

"This feels right," Liljeberg said and smiled at Katri. "There ought to be a big fuss when people move up in the world."

* * *

Anna phoned her childhood friend Sylvia, who lived in town. She couldn't think of anyone else to call now at a moment's notice.

"It's been a while," said Sylvia's well-modulated voice. "How is everything out there in the big woods?"

"Fine, everything is fine..." Anna was out of breath. They might be here any moment. Quickly and out of sequence she tried to tell her friend what had happened – Katri, Mats, the dog... Everything was about to change, everything...

"You don't mean you've taken boarders?" Sylvia said. "Surely you don't need to. I mean, you're quite well off, aren't you? By the way, are you working on anything, a new little tale?"

Sylvia's interest in her work had always been very important to Anna, but not right now. Anna replied snappishly that she never worked in the winter, which Sylvia ought to know, and then went headlong into her news about Katri while she tried to see down to the road through the veranda window.

"But dear Lord," said Sylvia in a pause. "You sound so *agitée*. Are you feeling well?"

"Yes, yes, I feel fine..."

Anna's friend began to describe some alterations she'd had done in her apartment and talked about the newly started Wednesday Society for Culture, which Anna really ought to join. And Anna should finally come to visit. It was important to get out and about, she knew that well enough, all the years she'd been a widow. "One shouldn't be alone, it leads to so much thinking..."

"But I'm not going to be alone!" Anna said. "That's what I'm trying to tell you! There are going to be four of us, didn't you hear me? Four of us, counting the dog..." Liljeberg's van was coming. "They're coming," she whispered. "I have to go..."

"Well, we'll talk again. Now take care of yourself and think twice before you do anything hasty. You cannot be too careful with boarders. I've heard so many stories. And as I said, drop by my little lair some day when you've got the time."

"Yes, yes, of course... Goodbye, I'll say goodbye now, goodbye..."

"Goodbye, little Anna."

They were coming up the hill. Anna stood close to the window and watched them come. Her heart had started pounding in a primitive impulse to get away, to just flee as far as the road would take her. So stupid. Why did she behave this way... and she'd been unpleasant to Sylvia, whom she liked so much and admired, had raised her voice and been impatient, although Sylvia was only being considerate and had even remembered to ask about her work... It had been a mistake to call. But it had felt absolutely necessary that someone she trusted should listen, listen carefully, and ask questions and maybe say, "But that sounds wonderful!" Or, "My dear Anna, what an exciting idea! You simply know what you want and go after it – just like that!"

* * *

Mats and Anna went up the stairs to the second floor. He said, "Can you believe it, Miss? I've never had my own room before."

"Haven't you? How remarkable. Now, what I thought was that if Katri took the pink room, you could have the blue. It was very popular in its day."

They stood in the door and looked. Mats said nothing.

Finally Anna said, "Don't you like it?"

"It's awfully nice. But you know, Miss, it's too big."

"How so, too big?"

"I mean, for one person. I'm not used to such a big room."

Anna was distressed. She explained that there weren't any smaller ones.

"Are you sure, Miss? When people build such big houses, they usually have some cubby-holes left over. They figure wrong and wind up with extra spaces under the roof."

Anna thought for a moment and said, "Well, we have the maid's room. But it's full of stuff, and it's always been too cold."

They went to the maid's room, and it really was very cold. Furniture, objects, things that had once been objects, odds and ends – all of it piled randomly up towards the angled ceiling, a chaotic jumble broken by a shaft of winter light from the window at the far end of the long, narrow room.

"This will be fine," Mats said. "Excellent. Where can I put all this stuff?"

"I don't really know... Are you sure you'd like to live in here?"

"Positive. But where shall I put all the stuff?"

"Wherever you like. Anywhere... I think I'll go lie down for a little while." The room had frightened Anna; it seemed threatening to her and tremendously melancholy. She went away, but the room followed. Very early images wandered through her head, images of the maid, Beda, who had been with them since she was a girl and had always lived in the dreadful room upstairs. Beda, who gradually became large and sleepy and who slept whenever she was free, just pulled up the covers and slept. How ghastly, Anna thought. I remember, they'd send me up when they needed her and every time she was just sleeping. What happened to her? Did she move away? Was she sick? I can't remember. And all that furniture: where did we have it? I didn't recognise it, but it must have been somewhere, it must have mattered. It must have been important to someone at some time...

Anna lay in her bed and stared at the ceiling. There was a little wreath of plaster roses around the light fixture on the ceiling, repeated in a long ribbon around the bedroom. She listened. Heavy objects were being dragged around upstairs and then dropped with a thud. Steps came and went, and silences that strained her hearing to the utmost. Now, again, something being dragged and dropped, everything up there changing places; all the past, which had rested above Anna Aemelin's bedroom as distant and undisturbed as the innocent dome of heaven, was in a state of violent transformation. All the same, Anna thought to herself, everyone has to have things the way they want them, and now I'm going to sleep. She pulled the pillow over her head, but sleep didn't come.

* * *

"But where is everything? How did you find the space?"

"We didn't," Katri said. "We carried a lot of it out on the ice, and Liljeberg took the rest of it to the auction house in town. He'll bring you the money if they can sell it. Though it probably won't be much."

"Miss Kling," said Anna, "are you sure you haven't acted a bit high-handedly?"

"Could be," Katri said. "But think about it, Miss Aemelin. What if we had presented you with every piece of discarded furniture, every single one of those sad objects, all those meaningless things? You would have stood there and tried to decide what should be saved or thrown out or sold. Now everything's decided and settled. Isn't that good?"

Anna was silent. "Probably," she said, finally. "But all the same, it was very high-handed."

Far out on the ice lay a dark pile of rubbish waiting for the ice to break up, a monument to Mama and Papa's complete inability ever to get rid of possessions. How remarkable, Anna thought. The ice will go, and everything will sink, just go straight down and disappear. It's bold, it's almost shameless. I have to tell Sylvia. Later it occurred to her that maybe it wouldn't sink, not all of it. Maybe it would float to another shore and someone would find it and wonder where it came from and why. In any event, it was not even the least bit Anna's fault.

13

SERENITY RETURNED TO THE RABBIT HOUSE. Mats moved as quietly as his sister, and Anna was never sure if he was at home. When they happened to meet in the house, Mats would stop, pause for a moment, smile, and bow his head before walking on – his own chivalrous gesture. Anna experienced some of the same shyness that Katri felt towards him. She never thought of anything to say at these encounters, and anyway she thought it unnecessary to bother him with the conventional greetings that people exchange on a staircase simply because they happen to be passing. Mats and Anna were together only in their books; everything else was an accepted no-man's-land.

Sometimes Anna heard hammering in the house, but she didn't go to investigate. As in the boat shed, Mats worked without being noticed and without showing his work. He just moved around, saw what needed fixing, and fixed it. There were many things in the rabbit house that had sagged or decayed or worn out – not a great deal;

it was just an old house that had started getting tired. It was only after a time that Anna noticed that a door didn't creak or a window could be opened, a draught was gone, a forgotten bulb was burning again – many small details that amazed and pleased her. Surprises, Anna thought, I love being surprised. When I was little, they'd hide Easter eggs all over the house for me to find, small, brightly coloured eggs with yellow feathers on them... You came in, you looked around, searched everywhere, and there was a bit of yellow fluff, sticking up just enough to be found...

Anna tried to thank Mats when they drank tea in the kitchen in the evenings, but she quickly realised that it only embarrassed him, so she stopped. They read their books, and all was well.

It was during this period that Anna began to be aware, in a new and disquieting way, of what she did with her time and what she didn't do. She began observing her own behaviour more and more with every day that passed – the days that had passed unexamined for so long. When Anna lived alone, she had not noticed how often she let the daylight hours vanish in sleep. Letting sleep come closer, soft as mist, as snow; reading the same sentence again and again until it disappeared in the mist and no longer had any meaning; waking up, finding your place on the page, and reading on as if only a few seconds had been lost. Now suddenly it was clear to Anna that she had slept, and for quite a long time. No one knew, no one disturbed her, but still the simple and irresistible need to vanish into a nap became a forbidden thing. She would wake up with a start, open her eyes wide, grab her book, and listen. It was completely quiet. But someone had walked across the floor upstairs.

Anna Aemelin no longer went to bed in the early evening, when it seemed more natural to follow the promptings of darkness and inclination than to follow the clock. Now she tried to stay awake. She would tramp around noisily in her room so they couldn't possibly get the impression upstairs that she had given up. And when Anna finally gave herself permission to go to bed, she couldn't sleep but lay awake listening. The house had a new secret life, and listening to its faint and indeterminate sounds was like trying to listen to an important but immensely distant conversation – catching a word here and a word there, but never getting a clear grasp of the context.

One evening when Anna couldn't sleep, she became very irritated, pulled on her dressing gown, stepped into her slippers, and shuffled out to the kitchen for a glass of juice and a sandwich. The dog lay by the kitchen door and followed her with his yellow gaze. The big animal lay as motionless as a sculpture and moved only his eyes. "Behave yourself," Anna whispered, making her usual detour. There were new rules in the refrigerator, everything wrapped in plastic so you couldn't tell what was what without unwrapping it.

For that matter, the whole kitchen was a new kitchen. What had changed, Anna could not discover, but in any case it was no longer her kitchen. Back in the days when everything was normal, if Anna got peckish in the middle of the night she would sometimes open a can of peas on the kitchen counter and eat them cold with a spoon while placidly contemplating the darkness in the back yard. Then she'd have a spoonful of jam and go quietly back to her bed. Now everything was different.

This evening, in the unimpeachable act of drinking juice, Anna took out the bottle with anxious haste as if she were doing something forbidden, poured without looking, and thick red syrup ran out over the counter. And of course there stood Katri. She had come in silently as always and stood watching what Anna was up to.

"I just wanted a little juice," Anna explained.

Katri said, "Wait, I'll clean it up." She took a rag, drenched it in red, and wrung it out in the sink.

"Let it be," Anna burst out. "It's water I want, just water!" And she opened the tap so violently that water splashed out on the floor.

Katri said, "Wouldn't it be nice to have a tray beside your bed at night?"

"No," Anna said. "I don't want it to be nice."

"But then you won't have to come out to the kitchen."

"Miss Kling," Anna said, "maybe I told you how Papa never wanted his paper delivered; he wanted to fetch it himself. Every day he picked up his paper at the shop and read it before anyone else. Throw that rag in the garbage bucket." Anna sat down at the table and repeated, "Throw it away. We throw things away that we no longer need."

"Miss Aemelin, does it disturb you, having us upstairs?"

"Not at all. I can't hear you. You're always sneaking around."

Katri was still at the sink. She took her cigarettes out of her pocket, remembered herself and put them back.

"Oh, go ahead," said Anna peevishly. "Smoke away. Papa smoked cigars."

When Katri had lit her cigarette, she said, slowly, groping for words, "Miss Aemelin, maybe we could look at this thing as a purely practical matter. We have made an agreement. Mats and I have gained greatly by this arrangement, but if you think about it, so have you. It's a kind of barter, reciprocal performance in kind. Certain services weighed against certain benefits. I know there are drawbacks, but they will lessen. We have to come to terms with it, accommodate to a voluntary contract. Couldn't we just accept it as a contract with rights and obligations?"

"'Reciprocal performance in kind,'" Anna repeated with exaggerated wonder, looking at the ceiling.

"A contract," Katri went on earnestly. "A contract is really much more remarkable than you might think. It doesn't just bind. I've noticed that for some people it's a relief to live with a contract. It frees them from indecision and confusion, they no longer have to choose. Both sides have agreed to share and assume responsibilities. It is, or ought to be, a deliberate promise where people have at least tried to be fair."

"I'm sure you're right," Anna said. "You're trying to be fair." She put her arms on the table to rest her back. She could feel sleep coming on.

"Fairness," Katri went on. "None of us ever knows absolutely for certain that we've managed to be fair and honest. But we try our best all the same..."

"Now you're preaching," Anna interrupted, standing up. "You know everything, my dear Miss Kling, but do you know what? We arrange things this way and that way, and in the final analysis we still have our tails behind us."

Katri started laughing.

"Mama used to say that," Anna said. "Sometimes when she got tired of explanations. Now I think I'll go to bed." In the door, she turned around. "Miss Kling, there's something I've been wanting to ask you. Don't you ever get upset and speak rashly?"

"I get upset," Katri said. "But I don't think I ever speak rashly."

Anna Aemelin got used to having her house invisibly inhabited. All her life she'd been getting used to things until they no longer seemed dangerous, and now she did it again. Soon she no longer heard the footsteps overhead, no more than she heard the wind and the rain and the parlour clock. The only thing she couldn't get used to was the dog. She still detoured around him and, once past, she would whisper to the motionless animal, expressing her fervent and unswerving opinion on some subject.

Anna had given the dog a name because nameless things have a tendency to grow. She stripped the animal of his menace by calling him Teddy. Anna knew perfectly well that she was not to interfere with the dog's strict training, so it was not out of kindness that she threw him scraps of food in secret. "Eat," she whispered. "Hurry up, little Teddy, and eat before she comes..." But sometimes as she passed his watchful yellow gaze, she would hiss, "Stay on your rug, you horrid great beast!"

14

"SYLVIA?" ANNA SHOUTED. "Is that you? I've tried to reach you again and again but you're always out... Is this a bad time? Do you have guests?"

"It's just my ladies," Sylvia said. "You know, it's Wednesday today."

"What Wednesday..?"

"The Culture Society," said Sylvia, over-articulating.

"Of course. Naturally... Can I call back later?"

"Call whenever you like; it's always nice to hear from you."

"Sylvia, could you come out here? I really mean it, could you come and visit..?"

"Of course I can," said Sylvia's voice. "It just never seems to happen. But sometime we really ought to get together and talk about old times. We'll see. Let's talk again, all right?"

Anna stood by the telephone for a long time and stared at the snowdrift through the window without seeing it. A great sadness gripped her. It can be sad having a friend you've admired too much and seen too rarely and told too many things that you should have kept to yourself. It was only to Sylvia that Anna had talked about her work – without reservation, boasts and cruel disappointments all jumbled together, everything. And now all of it was there with Sylvia, unloaded on her over the years in a dense clot of rash confidences.

I shouldn't have called, Anna thought. But she's the only one who knows me.

15

EMIL FROM HUSHOLM had his ice-fishing holes a couple of hundred metres out from the fishing shacks on shore. Sometimes his wife helped him check his nets and sometimes Mats. He always pulled up the nets himself, while whoever was with him let out the line. There was never much in them, a cod or two that they ate themselves. One day he was out with Mats, it was sleeting and fairly warm. He broke up the night ice around the edges of the hole, and Mats shovelled it out until the water was clean.

"Well, now," said Emil, "I've got a little surprise for you. This time you can pull up the net and I'll take care of the line. You ought to be able to handle that." The boy didn't seem to understand, so Emil went on. "I mean, I reckon you can at least pull up a net. I thought you might like to be trusted for once."

The insult dawned on Mats only slowly, and his gentleness made it sting all the more. Emil strode away to the other end of the net, where he was almost hidden by the sleet. Then he came back and stood ready and waiting, holding the line. Finally he shouted, "Well, are you just going to stand there? Can't you even pull up a net?"

Then fury rose up in Mats, the rare fury that only Katri knew about. He grabbed the end of the net rope and felt the net's living weight and stood still while his fury grew.

"Well?" roared Emil, who was also losing his temper. "Pull! Are you really the village idiot?"

Mats took out his knife and cut the rope in two, the net sank under the ice, and he turned and walked in towards the shore, past the huts and the boat shed, across the road, up the hill, and into the spruce woods behind the rabbit house. The snow was thawing, and at every step he sank in over his boots, then one boot caught and his foot came up wearing only a sock. He swore and drove his knife into the trunk of a tree, where it stuck and where it stayed.

Mats passed Anna in the hall, stopped for a moment and bowed his head in his usual gesture of respect. Anna did the same. As he moved on, Anna mentioned in passing that some new books had come from town.

There was much talk of the severed net. Emil said, "The poor boy's crazy. He's nice, but he's crazy; that much is crystal clear. I let him pull up the nets, because that's fun for a boy if there's fish, and he just stood there and sulked, and I got a little annoyed and hollered, that was all."

"I don't know how you dare have him in the boat shed," Fru Sundblom remarked, and the storekeeper chimed in to say that for all they knew that dimwit might chop up the boats, blood will out, you can't get around it.

"Now take it easy," Edvard Liljeberg said. "If Mats had his way, he'd handle those boats with velvet, that's how much he loves them. And whatever you give him to do gets done and done well, even if he is kind of slow. But you can give him any small job you like. I'll have a beer."

"In any case," Fru Sundblom cackled on, "the two of them come from bad stock. I'm not one to talk, but... I mean, how do you dare?"

"Oh, I think I dare," Liljeberg said. "I'll gamble on that boy. And on his sister. She may not always be so easy to deal with, but she's raised that boy. She's got courage and she's honest. What are you all so worked up about?"

"Oh, yes, indeed, she knows what she's doing," Fru Sundblom said. "Anyway, now they're sitting pretty. Old lady Aemelin is loaded."

"Shut up, you old bat," Liljeberg blurted out. His brother took his arm in warning, and Fru Sundblom jumped up from the table so suddenly she knocked over her coffee cup.

"There, you see," said Edvard Liljeberg. "Anyone can lose his temper and fly off the handle. But it's better than being mean. And so let me tell you something, all of you, and you can pass it on. The Klings are honest people, and whatever they do, they have their own good reasons."

And he left the shop.

16

"MISS KLING. It is very considerate of you to open my mail. But I have a little eccentricity that may strike you as childish – I enjoy opening envelopes. Like cutting the pages of a book or peeling an orange. It's just not the same once it's done."

Katri studied Anna with furrowed eyebrows that formed almost a single line above her eyes. "I understand," she said. "But I only open them to see what to throw out."

"But my dear Miss Kling," Anna said.

"You know, the things you don't need to bother with – advertisements, appeals, people who want money and are trying to cheat you."

"But how can you know?"

"I know. I feel it. I can smell flimflam a long way off, and I throw out everything that stinks."

Anna did not know what to say. Finally she pointed out that considerateness could go too far. Unfortunately, the damage was done, but in future Katri should set aside the rejected letters, to be looked at later.

"Where?"

"For example, somewhere in the attic..."

"Fine," Katri said and smiled. "Somewhere in the attic. And here are the bills from the shop. I've checked them thoroughly. He's cheating you systematically. Not much – fifty pennies here, one mark there – but he's doing it."

"The storekeeper? It's not possible." Anna looked with distaste at the bills, written in smudged blue ink, and pushed them away. "Yes, yes, I remember. You told me he was malicious, something about that liver... Fifty pennies here and fifty pennies there... But why him, why should he be specially malicious?"

"Miss Aemelin, this is important. I'm certain he's cheated you. Deliberately. Probably right from the start. Over time, it comes to a lot of money."

"Malicious?" Anna repeated. "When he's always been so friendly and polite..?"

"People are two-faced."

"But why should the storekeeper dislike me?" Anna said, with innocent amazement. "I'm so easy to like..."

Katri insisted. "Let's just talk about the bills. Believe me, they don't tally. I can count. We need to go into this."

"But why? Is it necessary? Don't you really just want to punish him?"

Katri observed tersely that Anna should do as she wished, of course, but that she needed to know what was going on.

"Yes, yes," said Anna calmly. "There are so many things a person might worry about." And she added, by

way of explanation, "What with one thing and another...
Don't you agree..?"

* * *

Anna Aemelin sat at her desk answering letters from
small children. She had arranged their letters in three
piles. Pile A was from the very young, who expressed
their admiration in pictures, mostly drawings of bunny
rabbits. If there was a written message, the child's mother
had written it. Pile B contained requests that were often
urgent, especially with regard to birthdays. Pile C was
what Anna called the Sad Cases pile, and these letters
required great care and reflection. But all three – A, B
and C – wanted to know how the rabbits got all covered
with flowers.

Anna had several explanations for her rabbits' flowery
fur, and they all seemed to work if she just got a good
start and didn't think too much. But today, for the first
time, Anna Aemelin couldn't come up with a single
reason – poetic, rational or humourous. The flowers were
simply an irrelevant phenomenon that seemed suddenly
silly and quite without charm. In the end, she just drew
rabbits, one rabbit on each letter, and afterwards covered
them all with flowers. But that was as far as she could go.
She waited a long time. She was thoroughly disgusted
with herself, and finally she got angry, put rubber bands
around A, B and C and carried them up to Katri.

The pink guest room was just as it used to be and yet
strange, maybe just larger and emptier. The window was

ajar and it was cold inside and smelled sour from cigarette smoke. Katri had been sitting and crocheting. Now she set aside her work and stood up.

"Do you like it in here?" asked Anna abruptly.

"Yes. Very much."

Anna walked towards the window, stopped, turned, and stood in the middle of the room with her letters in her hand.

"Shall I close the window?" Katri said.

"No. Miss Kling, those things you said about agreements... That both partners have rights and obligations. Look at these." Anna put her letters on the table. "The children ask question after question. Is it my obligation to answer? What rights do I have?"

"Not to answer," Katri said.

"I can't do that."

"But you have no agreement with them."

"How do you mean, 'agreement'..?"

"I mean a promise. You've written to each child only once, isn't that right? And you've made no promises."

"Well, as it happens..."

"You mean you've written to some of them more than once?"

"What am I supposed to do? They write and write, and they think I'm their friend..."

"Then it is a promise." Katri walked over and closed the window. "You're trembling," she said. "Miss Aemelin, sit down. I'll give you a blanket."

"I don't want one. And I haven't made any promises. I don't know what you mean."

"But look at it this way: You've taken something on. That means you have an obligation, doesn't it? Namely, that you'll do the best you can."

Anna was still standing in the middle of the room. She had started to whistle, a toneless, barely audible whistling through her teeth. Suddenly she said, angrily, "What's that?"

"I'm crocheting a coverlet."

"Oh, of course. Everyone crochets. I wonder how many beds there are in this village..."

Katri continued. "Agreements are all about fairness..." And Anna interrupted. "I've heard all that before. Both parties contribute and both parties gain. What does that have to do with my children? And what do I gain?"

"New editions. Popularity."

"Miss Kling," Anna declared, "I am popular."

"Or friendship, if you prefer. If friendship amuses you and you have time for it."

Anna gathered up her letters. "This wasn't at all what I wanted to talk about," she said.

"Leave them," Katri said. "Let me read them. I'll try to understand."

* * *

Later in the evening they sat opposite each other in the parlour and Katri explained. "I don't think this has to be so hard. The children have things to ask and things to tell, and what they all want is roughly the same. You could have a form letter, a prepared text in photostat.

When you need to vary it, you can add a postscript. And of course a personal signature."

"And you could sign them for me," Anna put in quickly.

"Yes, that would save you time. Or you could stamp the signature."

Anna sat up straighter. "Photostat? Form letter? It's not my style. And what happens if siblings write to me, or children in the same class in school, and they compare their letters? I can't possibly keep track of all the names and addresses."

"A card index would take care of that. And eventually you ought to have a secretary."

"A secretary!" Anna repeated. "A secretary! Is that what you think, Miss Kling? And what, for example, would she write to all the Sad Cases? For that matter, you've mixed up my piles, there was A, B and C... now I don't know which is which... How would a secretary answer 'Dear Miss Aemelin, what should I do with my parents?' Or 'Why does everybody get invited except me?' and so forth, on and on... It's me they're asking, not anyone else, and for that matter, they're all unhappy in their own way, and it seems to me they have a right to be!"

"I wouldn't be so sure," Katri said drily. "Miss Aemelin, I've read all these very carefully, and I can only conclude that A, B and C could all be included under a single heading. They all want something – for instance, comfort – and they want it as quickly as possible because it's very urgent. These letters could in fact be seen as small attempts at extortion. No, don't interrupt. Their letters are awkward and misspelled, and so they're touching and give you a bad conscience. But they'll learn, they'll get more proficient. And when they're grown up, many of them will write the letters that I help you throw away."

"I know. Out on the ice."

"No. Have you forgotten? Up in the attic."

After a moment's silence, Anna remarked threateningly that children can't be fooled, and she leaned back in her chair and whistled slowly between her teeth. Katri stood up and turned on the light. "You sentimentalise them because they're little," she said. "But the format doesn't matter. I have gradually learned that everyone, absolutely everyone of every size, is out to get something. People want things. It comes to them naturally. Of course they get more skilful with age, and they're no longer so disarmingly obvious, but the goal doesn't change. Your children simply haven't had time to learn how it's done. That's what we call innocence."

"And what is it Mats is out to get?" said Anna hotly. "Can you tell me that?" Without waiting for an answer, she went on. "This wasn't at all what I wanted to talk about, which is this: How did the rabbits get all covered with flowers?"

"Tell them it's a secret. Tell them they don't need to know."

"Exactly," said Anna. "You're right. That's the best thing you've said tonight. They don't need to know, and I don't want to know. So there!"

17

ANNA AEMELIN HAD A STANDING ORDER with the bookseller in town. Every now and then, he'd send books to her with Liljeberg – adventure stories, books about the seven seas and impassable landscapes and voyages of discovery undertaken by curious and intrepid men in the days when there were still anonymous white patches on the world map. Sometimes he sent classics and sometimes boys' books, but the general theme old Miss Aemelin had chosen never varied, and these books formed the unfailing linchpin of Mats and Anna's friendship.

The books came wrapped in brown paper, the address in yellow. Katri never opened them, just placed them on the kitchen table. Anna and Mats unpacked the books in the evening. Mats got first choice, and he always chose a book about the sea. When he'd read it, it went to Anna, and then they'd talk about it. It was a ritual. They said little about themselves or the things that happened around them. They spoke only about the people who lived in their books in a world of steadfast chivalry and ultimate justice. Mats never talked about his boat but often about boats.

* * *

Anna managed to forget the discarded letters that gradually accumulated somewhere in the attic, but one night they fluttered up in her dreams. She dreamed that she carried the unread letters out onto the ice, far out to the dark pile of abandoned but once cherished possessions, now shoved ruthlessly into a heap, and there she dumped them – the pleas of unknown correspondents, their confidences, their clever suggestions. She just threw them, and they flew away in a blizzard of letter paper, an endless, boundless postal storm, flew up to heaven in a single great reproach, and Anna woke up and jumped out of bed drenched with sweat and bad conscience.

She went out to the kitchen, the friendliest room in her house. The books still lay on the table, brand new, shiny in their tempting adventure colours. They smelled good. Anna raised one book after another to her cheek and inhaled the evanescent smell of unread book, unlike any other. She opened the lightly cleaving pages, which rustled at first touch, and studied the bold, stormy pictures, a vision of the improbable as the artist nevertheless imagined it. Anna did not believe this particular artist had ever experienced a real storm or wandered lost in a jungle. That's why, she thought. He makes it even more awful and terrible because he doesn't know. I doubt Jules Verne ever got to travel... I draw what I see. I don't have to yearn. Anna turned page after page and studied every illustration. Slowly, her anxiety abated.

The book dealer's bill was still on the table. Anna folded it again and again, held the paper in her fist and thought, this is a bill she'll never get to see. Somehow she'd surely figure out that the bookseller is cheating me too.

* * *

After the net incident with Husholm's Emil, Mats stopped doing odd jobs in the village, but he went to the Liljebergs' boat shed as usual. There no one talked about anything but boats, when they talked at all. When they closed for the day, Mats went home to his boat designs. The walls in his room had once been blue like most of the house, now they had faded to the indefinable colour of an old blue leather binding or bluebells in a herbarium. The damp had stained and bleached the narrow room with its angled ceiling, and Mats thought the walls and ceiling looked like a sky with flying storm clouds.

He was very happy. There was nothing unnecessary in his room. The window was small and looked out on the woods. Huge old spruce trees filled the view like a dark, snow-flecked wall. It was like being alone in the boat shed. Katri had put one of her crocheted coverlets on the bed. It too was blue, but clear blue, like a signal. As always, Mats slept without dreaming and never woke up in the night.

Katri did not see much of her brother, mostly just at meals. The quiet silence of kinship that had been theirs had lost its particular time and space. Sometimes in the evening Katri had some errand to the kitchen. Mats and Anna sat across from each other at the kitchen table and read. They always stopped reading while Katri was in the room, but they no longer asked her if she'd like a cup of tea.

18

ANNA WAS VERY ANNOYED. She had spent an entire day trying to put together a form letter, a perfect letter that would answer, inform, comfort and suit every child. But however much she tried, it sounded more and more stilted.

"Look at this," she said. "Just look at it, Miss Kling! Do you see now that I was right?"

Katri read the letter and said that it seemed unclear and that it failed to suggest in any way that all future correspondence was cordially discouraged.

"But don't you understand that the whole idea is impossible? Every child needs a personal letter."

"I understand. You'll just have to do it your own way."

Anna put on her glasses, then took them off again and polished them for a long time. She said, "I don't know what's the matter with me, but I can't write letters any more. It doesn't feel right."

"But haven't you been writing them for years? I mean, you're a writer."

"That's all you know!" Anna said. "It's the publisher puts together the text. I draw the pictures, you know, the pictures! Have you even seen them?"

"No," Katri said. She waited, but Anna said nothing. "Miss Aemelin, I have a suggestion. Could you give me a couple of the letters and let me answer them? As an experiment?"

"You can't write," said Anna quickly. Then she shrugged her shoulders, stood up from the table and left the room.

* * *

With the same ease that Katri Kling could duplicate signatures, she could also imitate voices and another person's choice of words and manner of speech. It was a talent that had gone begging. She had occasionally tried to amuse Mats by mimicking the neighbours, but he didn't like it.

"They're too real," he said.

"How so?"

"I see how awful they are."

Katri stopped playing a game that wasn't fun. But in the letters from Anna, her talent was put to use. Easily and skilfully, she reproduced Anna's uncertainty and her awkward kindness getting lost in needless small talk. Beneath the kindness there were still glimpses of egocentricity. But gone was the timid inability to say no. There were no more half-promises that might tempt some youngster to become a penpal. Katri bid them an honest farewell that only an unusually stupid or blindly ingenuous child could misunderstand. Anna read through what Katri had written and was bewildered. It was her voice but not her voice, a distorted picture that came closer and closer with each letter she read until she set the whole pile aside and sat silently for a long time.

It was a peculiarity of Katri's that silence never made her ill at ease. She just waited. Finally Anna picked up the letters again, searched through them, fastened her eyes on Katri, and said, "This is wrong! Here you're not me! If a child is mad at her parents, it's no comfort that the parents may be having troubles of their own. That's the wrong comfort! I never would have written that. Parents have to be strong and perfect or the child can't believe in them. You'll have to fix it."

Katri's reaction was suddenly vehement. "But how long can they rely on what's not reliable? For how many years do we fool these children into believing in something they shouldn't believe in? They have to learn early, or they'll never manage on their own."

"I've managed on my own," said Anna tartly. "And done very nicely. And look at this one: you say that sooner or later every child gets mad at his parents and it's natural. Do you think I could have written that?"

"No, that was a mistake. There I wasn't being you."

"No, that wasn't nice. If all children get mad, then that particular child is less important. He's just like all the other children."

"Well, maybe, but they move in packs," Katri said. "They do their best to be all alike. It's a comfort to them that all the others behave the same way."

"But some of them are individualists!"

"It's possible. But then they need to hide in the pack all the more. They know if they're different they'll be chased away."

"And what about this one?" Anna went on. "Where's the chitchat? He's tried to draw a rabbit – obviously no talent at all – so here you could write something like 'I've hung your picture above my desk'... This one's learning to skate, and her cat's name is Topsy. You can fill nearly a whole page with the skating and the cat if you write big enough. You're not using the material."

"Miss Aemelin," said Katri, "you're actually quite cynical. How have you managed to hide that?"

Anna wasn't listening. She put her hand on the pile of letters and declared, "More affection! Bigger writing! And talk about my own cat: describe it, talk about it..."

"But you don't have a cat."

"That doesn't matter. The whole point is to give them a nice letter... You have to learn how it's done. But I wonder if you can. I almost think you don't like them."

Katri shrugged her shoulders and smiled her quick wolfish smile. "Neither do you," she said.

Anna's annoying blush rose over her cheeks, and she put an end to the conversation. "What I think has no significance. But they need to believe in me, to know I could never deceive them. And now I'm tired."

* * *

Oh, Anna Aemelin, the only thing you care about is your own conscience. That's what you cherish. You're a charming little liar. A child writes, "I love you, I'm saving my money to come and live with you and the bunnies," and you answer, "How lovely. You'll be very welcome." And it's a lie. The promises made by a guilty conscience acknowledge and settle no debts... You can't hide. In the long run, you can't even try to make it easier for yourself by not daring to say no, by kidding yourself that everyone in the final analysis is nice and can be kept at a distance with promises or money... You know nothing about fair play! You're a difficult opponent. The truth needs to be hammered in with iron spikes, but no one can drive nails into a mattress!

* * *

Relief at not having to write letters to children dug an unexpected hole in Anna's well-regulated day, which became easy and empty and difficult to fill. But she continued to add her beautiful signature and to draw a rabbit at the bottom of every reply Katri placed before her. One day, when Anna was tired, Katri made a slip. She signed the letters and drew the rabbits herself. They were pictured from behind, sitting in the grass, which made it easier. Nevertheless, Katri's rabbits were boldly and carelessly drawn. Anna looked at them and said nothing, but her glance was as cold as the whirling snow outside the house, and Katri drew no more rabbits.

* * *

Anna called Sylvia a couple of times, but there was no answer.

19

OCCASIONALLY PEOPLE STILL CAME to Katri for advice on some perplexing problem, but it happened only rarely. They didn't like going up to the rabbit house on their own business. It somehow made their private affairs too visible. Of course it was Katri who answered the door when they rang the bell, but old Miss Aemelin would come rushing up behind her like a startled bird and stand looking over Katri's shoulder, wondering what it was about and whether she should make some coffee or maybe not or maybe tea. It felt all backwards, and when they finally climbed the stairs to Katri's room, it seemed almost shameful, like sneaking out to ask a fortune teller for advice. It was at about this time that the children started shouting 'witch' when Katri passed – wherever they'd got that idea. Children smell things in the air, like little dogs. They were silent as Katri walked by, and then, with one voice, and in a monotone, they'd start chanting.

This time she went into the shop. The dog waited outside and the children were quiet.

The storekeeper asked how everything was at the rabbit house.

"Fine, thank you," said Katri.

"So Miss Aemelin is well? Has the old lady written her will?"

They were alone in the shop. Katri was searching the shelves, and she asked if he had any of that hearth bread, the soft kind.

"No. Has she lost her bite? Or her nerve?"

Katri said, "Be careful. I'm warning you."

But he couldn't stop. "It's others have the teeth these days." He hurled it towards her. "Right?"

Katri swung around, and her eyes were wide open and pure yellow. "Watch it!" she said. "The dog will do what I tell him. And he has teeth."

She paid and walked towards home with the dog. Behind her, the children continued their monotonous hate song. Mats came walking down the village street and stopped suddenly when he heard the children chanting 'witch'. His face went white.

"Let it go," said Katri. "They're harmless."

But her brother walked slowly towards the children, his hands hanging down but open as if to grab, and the children fled, silently.

"Let it go," Katri said again. "You know you have to be careful about losing your temper. There's no need. I don't let anything bother me."

* * *

That same evening, Liljeberg came to the rabbit house and wanted to talk to Katri about a dispute with the storekeeper. They went upstairs to her room.

"It's this business with the van," Liljeberg said. "He pays for the petrol and gives me a discount on what I buy in the shop, but I want more pay. I've checked with drivers in town, and they get more. Now he's saying that if I insist on a pay rise, then someone else can drive the van."

"Is there anyone else in the village who could do it?"

"Yes, one or two. And they'd work for less just because they think it's fun."

"How big is your discount, and what's your pay?"

Liljeberg pulled out a piece of paper and handed it to her. "This is what I get, and this is what I want. And he won't give in."

Katri said, "There's one thing you may not know. He doesn't pay for the petrol The government pays petrol for hauling the gas cannisters from the fish pier out to the lighthouse. But they don't know it's a two-minute drive. And they don't know he gets an extra allowance from the post office and hauls his goods in the mail van. He's given them the wrong information, and they could take away his licences if they wanted to."

Liljeberg said nothing for quite a while. Then he asked carefully how Katri could be so sure.

"I did the accounts in the shop for quite some time."

"I'll be damned," said Liljeberg and was silent again. Finally he observed that it would be almost like extortion. The storekeeper might be double-dealing, but you couldn't go ratting to the authorities; it was simply unthinkable.

"Do what you like. Just let him know that you know what's going on. He'll raise your salary."

"Well, if you say so. But it isn't something I like doing. But thank you anyway."

When Liljeberg had gone, Katri went on with her coverlet. There wasn't a sound in the house. Katri crocheted quickly without looking at the work that occupied her hands. Crocheting was mostly a way of resting her thoughts. But they came nevertheless, one after the other, until she suddenly bent over under the weight of a single implacable insight that struck her as dreadful. She needed to talk to Liljeberg again, now, at once. She rushed down to the hall, threw on her coat, and motioned the dog to follow. It was already dark. In her hurry, she'd forgotten her torch, but she didn't take the time to go back.

The short cut to the Liljebergs was not tramped down, and again and again she walked right into trees, stopped for a moment, then trudged ahead with her arms stretched out ahead of her. She could smell the Liljebergs' rabbit farm before she could make out the window through the trees. The lighted rectangle spread a pale light across the snow. They were probably eating their supper. She should have waited for morning; she was behaving badly, but it couldn't be helped, and it didn't matter. Katri left her boots on the porch. Edvard Liljeberg himself opened the door. His brothers were having their evening meal.

"There was something I wanted to say," Katri said. "It won't take long. I'll wait."

"No need," Liljeberg said. "My dinner will keep. Let's go in the small parlour."

The parlour was very cold; the brothers all slept in the big room. Katri didn't want to sit. Hastily and harshly she explained. "I was wrong. Your salary is normal, and your discount on food almost on the high side. He probably has cheated people here and there, but he hasn't cheated you. So I take back what I said. I was being unfair."

Edvard Liljeberg was embarrassed. He offered her a cup of coffee, but she thanked him no. Before she left, she said, "Just remember one thing: Going along with something doesn't mean you give in to it. Keep an eye on him. And whatever else, you're still the winner, because you like driving the van, and he doesn't know that."

The powerful rabbit smell struck Katri as she came out into the yard. Now it was done. Maybe Liljeberg wouldn't trust her any more, and that would be very bad. It was from the Liljebergs she would order Mats's boat, and she would have to order it soon if they were to finish it by summer. No one could make Liljeberg believe in money that didn't yet exist, or in the promise of a person who had put her honesty in question by losing her way on the straight path she had so inexorably staked out.

20

Winter now entered a new phase. The shoreline was silent. Out on the ice, the wind had opened glassy patches between long strips of snow. There was a lot of ice fishing, and Emil from Husholm's red snowmobile could sometimes be seen on its way to ice holes further out, his wife behind him on a toboggan. The snowdrifts shrank and grew fragile, but the ice was still strong, even in the bay and around the headlands. And day after day, the weather was clear.

One morning, Anna went down to the fish pier and looked out across the ice trying to catch sight of the big pile of furniture that Katri had condemned to sink, but the light from the sky blinded her and she saw nothing. Hammering came from the boat shed, two men hammering in a regular rhythm that stopped simultaneously and then started again. Anna sat down on a tub and closed her eyes in the sun.

"Beautiful day," said Katri behind her. "You forgot your sunglasses."

Anna thanked her and stuffed the sunglasses in a pocket.

"And the mail has come. Another letter from the plastics company."

Anna's back stiffened and she closed her eyes even tighter. Finally she remarked that the sun was beginning to feel warm, and she started to whistle softly to herself. Katri stood where she was a short while, before going back to the rabbit house.

* * *

Anna had managed to forget the plastics company, along with so much else. What she called the brown envelopes, typewritten, never decorated with flowers, had cast a shadow on her life for far too many years. For the most part, Anna got away with thanking them for their interest, how nice it was her rabbits could be put to use, yes the terms were acceptable, cordially yours. But sometimes they were difficult; sometimes they wanted information, facts that Anna couldn't locate in her memory or in the drawers of her cabinet. Then in cowardly despair she would put the troublesome letters in the Drawer for Further Consideration and somehow manage to forget them.

Of course the plastics company should have gone the same route. They had written several weeks earlier asking for copies of every contract she had ever signed relating to the rabbits. Anna was on her way to the cabinet just as Katri started beating rugs outside in the yard. Anna stopped with the letter in her hand, then went back and read it several times, but there was nothing in it she might have misunderstood. In the end, she opened several drawers in her large cabinet at random and every drawer was chock-full of letters and unintelligible papers. It seemed the most natural thing in the world to close them again and hide herself in a book.

But the next morning, she was seized by this new kind of conscience, and the plastic company's "as soon as possible" burned right through the envelope in fiery letters. Hastily, so she wouldn't have time to change her mind, Anna emptied several drawers on her bed and started rooting through the letters. She quickly realised that she had to sort them into piles. The bed wasn't big enough, and piles began tumbling to the floor and getting mixed up. She had to continue on the rug. And it was impossible to remember which pile was which, so she was constantly putting letters in the wrong pile, and her back hurt. As noon approached, she went after Katri.

"Look what a mess they've caused me," she said. "They want to see all my contracts! How am I supposed to know where they are? And on top of everything, Mama's and Papa's letters are mixed up with mine, every Christmas card and every receipt since the eighteen hundreds!"

"Is there more of this?"

"The whole cabinet is full. The stuff I thought I didn't need is there higher up. Or maybe in the middle…"

"And they're in a hurry?"

"Yes."

"They'll have to wait," Katri said. "This will take some time. But I think I'm pretty good at organising."

Mats carried everything up to Katri's room, and the cabinet was empty. To Anna it felt like a great defeat, but her relief was even greater.

* * *

Briskly and with increasing amazement, Katri began to sort through the deluge of confusion that an inattentive, impractical person can produce if given enough time. Katri read here and there and began to suspect the worst, but at the moment she had only to find the contracts. When she did find them, she saw that they could not be shown to anyone. No rational person, seeing how profoundly Anna had let herself be cheated, could ever be induced to offer her better terms. Katri explained this to Anna.

"But they're waiting," Anna objected. She was very anxious.

"They'll have to wait. We'll write and say we're expecting their offer as soon as possible."

"But what do we say about the contracts? Maybe that we've lost them?"

"Contracts don't get lost. Why should we lie? We'll say nothing."

* * *

It was then the brown folders came into the house. Katri had them sent from town. She stopped crocheting.

Evening after evening, with great care, she went over the draughts of Anna's business letters. They were undated, and the pages, never numbered, were often found in different drawers. With patience and something of the instinct of a hunting dog, Katri figured most of it out. All her life, she'd had a strong need for clarity, for putting everything in order, and working with Anna Aemelin's letters gave her a sense of calm fulfilment. As time went by, Katri got a pretty clear picture of what had transpired over a very long period of time, and she began doing the maths. She added up the sums that Anna Aemelin had lost by being almost criminally credulous or quite simply careless and lazy. Some of it could be written off to an unwillingness to say no, or to social conscience, but less than she might have expected. Mostly, Anna had simply not cared. Katri wrote the lost sums in a black notebook.

"How's it going?" Anna asked in the door. "Dear Miss Katri, I'm afraid I've been a bit careless..."

"Yes, unfortunately. You've made very imprudent agreements. There's not much here we can rescue." While Katri went on about percentages and guaranteed minimums, Anna stood in sullen silence before the line of brown folders, each of which had a square label in her own lovely handwriting telling what it contained. She wasn't listening. The folders depressed her. It was as if everything she'd done and left undone had suddenly been itemised and laid out in implacable order for all and sundry to consider and disparage.

Suddenly Katri interrupted herself and said, "Stop whistling."

"Was I whistling?"

"Yes, Miss Anna. You whistle all the time. Please don't. Anyway, as I was saying, now that you have these folders, this will all be much easier. You can find what you need right away and get a clear picture of the situation."

Anna gave Katri a long look and said, "The situation..."

"Your business situation," said Katri, slowly and amiably. "Your agreements. What you've said and what they've said. For example, you need to know what percent they gave you last time if you're going to ask for more. Right?"

"And what's that you have on the floor?" said Anna suddenly.

"I'm sewing them together into a coverlet. I'm trying to get the colours to go together."

"Oh, yes. Getting the colours to go together." Anna picked up one of the crocheted squares laid out on the floor and studied it closely. She turned away and said, brusquely, that it had been very nice of Katri to organise her correspondence because now they could find anything, supposing they wanted to find it, which she hoped would not be necessary, since, all things considered, it was all water under the bridge.

"That's true," said Katri sternly. "It's water under the bridge. And the water will keep coming unless someone does something about it." She paused for a moment and then asked, "Anna, do you trust me?"

"Not particularly," said Anna sweetly.

Katri started to laugh.

"You know what, Katri?" Anna said, turning around. "Somehow I like you better when you laugh than when you smile. This coverlet is a fine piece of work, but the green is in the wrong place. Green is a very difficult colour. And now I think a nice walk would feel good. Why don't you bring Teddy along and give him a little air?"

Katri's face closed again. "No," she said. "You're not good for that dog. He only goes out with me or with Mats."

Anna shrugged her shoulders and, with sudden spite, commented that Katri's interest in money seemed somewhat exaggerated. In her family, money was not considered a proper topic of discussion.

"Really?" Katri said. The word came out like a blow. "You don't say! An improper topic?" She had gone pale, and she took an uncertain step towards Anna.

"What's the matter?" Anna said, backing away. "Don't you feel well?"

"No, I don't feel well. I feel really ill when I see how you throw money down the drain for no reason at all. Because what you throw away, what you so utterly despise, is quite simply possibilities. Don't you understand? The possibility of becoming so secure you don't have to think about money, the possibility of being generous, the potential for new ideas that can't grow without money. Without money, a person's thinking gets narrow. It shrivels! You have no right to let them cheat you this way..." Katri had been speaking in a very quiet voice – a new, frightening voice – and now she stopped. The silence stretched on and grew awkward.

"I don't understand," Anna said.

"No. You don't understand."

"You're so pale. Is there anything I can do..?"

"Yes, there is something you can do," Katri said. "You can let me manage your affairs. I know how. I do. I can double your income." When the silence descended again, she added, "I beg your pardon. I've said too much."

"Indeed," said Anna. "But you seem to be feeling better." She was using her mother's voice, that long-gone, benevolent, supercilious voice. "My dear Katri, you may do precisely as you like. But you mustn't get the idea that I am in any way deficient in security or generosity. And my ideas, I can assure you, are quite independent of my income." Anna gave Katri a little nod, a slight flexure of the neck, and left the room. On the stairs, she felt suddenly exhausted and had to stop for a moment. Then it passed.

"Rashly?" Anna whispered contemptuously. "Rashly? She, Katri, who thinks she never speaks rashly? And what did she mean? What is it that's my fault?"

Downstairs the dog lay glaring at her with his yellow eyes, the superior, dangerous dog that she was not to touch or feed. For the first time, Anna went straight over to the big animal and clapped him on the head, and it was a powerful clap that was anything but friendly.

* * *

"Dear Sirs, We regret that Miss Aemelin has not had an earlier opportunity to answer your query of the..." Katri looked at the query. It was two years old, but maybe it wasn't too late. The offer was very advantageous. Katri set down her pen and stared blankly out the window. Beside her on the table she had a *Guide to Business Correspondence* and an English dictionary. The letters in English were difficult, but she managed. Teeth clenched, Katri wrote her stumbling but exceedingly explicit letters to the people who, for their various reasons, saw the flowery rabbits as a source of profit.

The unavoidably simple wording of the letters gave them an air of finality that was almost brutal. Every time Katri managed to inflate a fee or trade a one-time payment for a royalty, she noted her success in the black notebook. She also noted down the amounts preserved by saying no to all sorts of charities, amateur enthusiasms, and general cries for help from imprac-tical but obstinate individuals. Everything was written into the notebook, every penny honourably recorded. Katri told herself it was money she had earned for Mats by not giving in and never rashly asking for too much. The answers she got to her letters were cold but respectful, and very rarely did she have to modify her demands. Neither party added a polite closing sentence about the weather.

On the cover of the black notebook, Katri pasted a label on which she wrote "For Mats". This serious game of challenging and recovering became a utilitarian game of hazard that occupied her thoughts continu-ously. Katri was in the grip of the collector's peculiar mania. Every time she wrote a captured sum of money into her notebook, she felt the collector's deep satisfaction at finally owning a rare and expensive specimen. Scrupulously, Katri worked out what should rightfully belong to Anna and what could belong to Mats. Into Anna's pot she put whatever Anna herself would have accepted. Of what Katri managed to recover or repair, Anna got two-thirds. But when it came to people who wanted something without offering anything in return, the whole profit went to Mats. There were borderline cases where Anna's pliancy could have meant additional sales over the long run, and these Katri divided evenly.

* * *

"So the plastics company is all set," Katri said. "It went better than I expected. And their option won't collide with United Rubber."

"Really," Anna said.

"There's another letter from your publisher."

Anna read it and remarked that it wasn't as friendly as usual.

"Of course not. They know they can't cheat you any more. We want a royalty next time instead of a flat fee. I hope you haven't given them an option for future books."

"Maybe. I don't remember exactly..."

"There's nothing about it in your papers. For that matter, you should think about changing publishers if they won't give you better terms."

Anna straightened up, but before she could say anything, Katri continued. "Here's an amateur theatre that wants to use flowery rabbits. They paint the flowers themselves. They don't have any money, but they charge for the tickets. I've suggested a very small royalty."

"No," said Anna flatly. "Nothing at all."

"They've agreed to two percent. We can't change our position. Here's a textile company, three percent, I've raised it to five. Probably wind up at three-and-a-half, four tops. No, don't say it. They just lose respect if we don't try. And this is United Rubber again. They want to reduce the royalty so they can put a speaker in the rabbits. It will be expensive, but they'll raise the price. What can we accept?"

"What do they say?"

"Three percent."

"No, I mean the rabbits."

"The letter doesn't tell."

"Rabbits don't make sounds. Though I think they squeal if they're scared. Or when they die."

"Please, Anna. This is work we have to do. A job."

"Yes and no," Anna burst out. "I don't want a squealing rabbit, it's ridiculous."

"But you don't ever have to see it. It's going to squeal somewhere in Central Europe. And nobody there knows you, and you don't know them."

"What do they want to give us?"

"Three percent."

"Two!" Anna shouted and leaned across the table, her neck turning bright red. "Two percent! One percent for me, and one for you."

Katri was silent. When her silence continued, Anna understood that she'd said something important. She repeated it. "One for me and one for you. We'll share. We'll share Central Europe." It sounded adventurous. She said it again. Katri drew a deep breath and said, with a certain chill, that it was out of the question. But if Anna had no objection, they could assign half the royalty from United Rubber to Mats.

"Do so," said Anna. "That's fine. And not another word about United Rubber, ever."

Katri opened the black notebook and, in her own sweeping hand, wrote, "Mats 1%".

"Is there anything else of importance?"

"No, Anna," Katri said. "We've done what matters most."

21

AT TWILIGHT, just as work in the boat shed stopped for the day, Katri walked down to the fish piers. The wind was blowing hard again. The Liljeberg brothers were walking home, and Katri met them. She stopped in front of Edvard Liljeberg. The others walked on.

"It's blowing so hard," Katri said. "Could we get out of the wind for a moment?"

"I don't know," Liljeberg answered. "What's it about?" He recalled their last conversation quite clearly, and he was a little wary of her.

"It's about a boat. I want to order a boat."

Liljeberg just looked at her. So Katri shouted into the wind, "A boat! I want you to build a boat for Mats!"

He didn't answer but turned back to the shed and unlocked the door. Katri had never been inside. The wind was making a racket against the metal roof, but the vast room seemed hugely calm and peaceful. The hull of a boat under construction was visible in the half-light, its giant ribcage in silhouette against the far wall of windows.

Broad boards that would soon be planking hung in bundles from the ceiling, and there was a smell of shavings and tar and turpentine. Katri understood why her brother always wanted to come back here to this protected world where everything was correct and clean. She turned to Liljeberg and asked if he had time for a large boat with a cabin.

"How large?"

"Nine and a half metres. Carvel-built."

"We may very well have time. But it's likely to be expensive. What about the motor?"

"A four-cylinder paraffin engine," Katri answered. "A forty- or fifty-horsepower Volvo Penta. Mats has done the boat designs. I think they look good. Though I know nothing about boats."

"It sounds like you know quite a bit," said Liljeberg.

"I've gone through his notes."

"Well, well, yes, he ought to know a thing or two by now. Maybe I could have a look at those drawings."

"There's just one small difficulty," Katri said. "I don't want Mats to know about this until I'm sure."

"You mean sure you can pay for it."

Katri nodded.

"And can you?"

"Yes. But not now. Later in the spring."

"I have to say", Liljeberg said, "that, everything considered, this is a pretty strange order. What am I going to tell the others? There has to be a purchaser. Is it Miss Aemelin?"

"No. No, it's not."

"And you don't want to figure in this?"

"No. Not yet."

"Listen here," said Liljeberg, looking her straight in the eye. "What is it you want me to do? Am I supposed to tell stories on your behalf because you can't do it yourself?"

Katri didn't answer. She walked over to the wall where the tools hung, gleaming, each in its own rack, in perfect order. Tentatively, she touched one tool after the other. Just like her brother, Liljeberg thought. They take things in their hands the same way. I can't give her away. With this kind of dubious order in the works, they'll be all over her again, the little witch. And if she can't pay for it, I'm sure I can sell it to someone else. He said, quite brusquely, "Let's go. I'll see what I can do."

* * *

Later that evening, Liljeberg came to the rabbit house and asked for Mats. He'd heard something about plans for a boat, and he wanted to have a look at them. They went through the drawings together. "That's very good, right in here," he said. "But there's room for improvement. Bring these with you in the morning. But don't tell anyone."

At home, he said they'd received an order for a carvel-built, nine-and-a-half metre, and the purchaser wanted to remain anonymous.

"And when did you hear about this?"

"A while ago," Liljeberg said, and the lie came easily, like a gift to someone you value.

22

ANNA HAD GROWN QUIET AND SULLEN. A nasty suspicion had taken hold of her, namely, that she, a kind and friendly person, had been thoroughly cheated. For the first time in her life, Anna became distrustful, and the feeling did not agree with her or with those around her. She went around brooding about all of them – neighbours, publishers, innocent little children, everyone. Absolutely everyone had cheated her.

She dug back in time and stopped only when she got to Papa and Mama. And, of course, Sylvia. Everything outside the rabbit house became an uncertain world of pettiness and secret ridicule. No one respects gullible people, Katri had said. And now Katri sat there again with her papers and her patient, insistent voice urging Anna to listen, to stop working against her own interests by simply saying no before she even knew what it was all about, because this time there was a large sum of money involved, and think what you could do with so much money if only you could see how much more it might become if the party of the second part could be made to deal honourably, and so forth, and so on.

"Katri," Anna said, "now listen to what I'm going to tell you. It's this: that I would much rather be cheated than to go around distrusting everyone."

Then Katri made a mistake. "But it's too late for that, isn't it?" she said. "You can't make that choice, because you already don't trust them any more. Isn't that right?"

Anna stood up from the table and left the room. In the hall, she opened wide the door to the yard and then walked right over to Katri's dog and whispered, "Get out of here!" Her hands could feel the big animal's powerful muscles under his rough coat, but Anna was not afraid. She gave the dog a substantial shove and got him out in the snow. She grabbed a stick from the woodpile and threw it as far as she could, shouting, "Fetch! Retrieve!" The dog just looked at her without moving. Anna threw another stick. "Fetch! Play! Do as I tell you!" She was sobbing with rage. It was very cold. When she went back inside, she left the door wide open.

* * *

Anna persisted. Every time she knew the house was empty, she chased the dog outdoors. Stubbornly, teeth clenched, she threw sticks into the woods, time after time, day after day. Finally the dog retrieved one, very slowly, then drew aside with his ears laid back and stood motionless in the snow and stared at her.

"What are you doing?" asked Mats, who had come up the hill and stopped at the corner of the house.

"Teddy's playing," Anna said, startled. "All dogs like to retrieve..."

"Not this one," Mats said. "He's not allowed to take orders from anyone but Katri. Come inside." Mats had never before spoken to Anna sternly. He held the door open and she walked quickly past him into the hall.

New books had arrived. "Take whatever you like," Anna said. "But I don't want to read this evening."

Mats picked up the books one after another and put them down again. Finally he said anxiously that trained dogs were different, you couldn't upset them and confuse them. You had to be careful with them. Katri had never made the dog retrieve.

"But that dog is unhappy."

"I don't know about that," Mats said. "He's got a pretty good life in a way. And anyhow I think it's too late to change him at this stage."

"Well, which book do you want?" said Anna impatiently. "Let me see what they've sent... *Little Erik's Sea Voyage*. Outrageous. Looks like they're just sending junk they want to get rid of. I might have known... Have you read Joseph Conrad? *Typhoon*?"

"No."

Anna went to get it. "Here you are. For once, read something that's true to life. *Typhoon* is the best thing ever written about a ship in a storm. It's much more than an adventure. More than a storm... Believe me, even your literary sister may have read Joseph

Conrad." After a moment or two she added, "If she understood it."

Mats avoided looking at Anna. He opened the book, turning the pages with the same care he took with everything he touched, and mentioned cautiously that Katri understood most things, she was very smart. "Much smarter than us," he said.

"That's possible," Anna said. "But speak for yourself. One thing I do know, my young friend, she's not gifted. That's another thing entirely."

When Anna had gone, Mats made himself a cup of tea, sat down at the kitchen table and began to read. The house became silent in the storm.

* * *

Anna had lost her desire to read. The heroes of sea, jungle and wilderness were suddenly just lifeless images. They no longer afforded her entry to an honourable world of just deserts, eternal friendship and rightful retribution. Anna did not understand how this had happened, and she felt herself shut out.

One day Anna declared, quite casually, that in future she wanted to have nothing whatsoever to do with business; she didn't want to talk about it or know about it. Katri, who knew so much about percentages, could allocate them however she wished.

"But Anna, I can't do that. I can't take responsibility for your most important letters. This is serious. We're not playing at this, like a game."

"No, you're incapable of playing," said Anna a bit cruelly. "You don't know how to play – that's precisely the problem."

* * *

It was about this time that Katri worked out her game of playing for percentages, which she called the Mats Game. It was very simple. Cardboard squares, each with a clearly lettered percentage – '5%', '4½%', '7%', '10%', etcetera – which she dealt out like playing cards. The game was played quickly and without a lot of rules.

Katri: "These people bid four percent. What do we bid?"

Anna, throwing a card on the table: "Five percent. Don't let them cheat us!"

"And how much for Mats?"

"Two and a half."

Katri: "No, I'll trump that. Four for you and two for Mats. But you picked up one percent by raising to five. We'll put that in the kitty."

"And what do we do with the kitty?"

"You decide."

Anna, laughing: "A coverlet for Teddy. Okay. Next bid?"

"They're proposing seven and a half."

Anna: "Ten! But only four for Mats."

"Anna, you're cheating. You don't have the ten."

"Okay, eight then. But Mats still gets four, like I said. No, five. Five percent."

And Katri wrote it down.

Her opponent leaned back in her chair and said, "Okay, next?"

"There isn't anything else this time. We've answered everything I found in the cabinet."

"But we could pretend," Anna said. "I want to go on."

They started playing for fictitious amounts, usually when it started getting dark. They would build a fire, light two candles on the table, set out pen and paper, deal, bid and throw down cards, each representing huge sums that could gradually grow to millions. Katri kept score. She humoured Anna by playing this new millions game, and she usually let Anna win, but its make-believe quality tormented her. It seemed to infringe on the dignity of real numbers. When the game had been about Anna's business affairs, or, rather, about Anna's way of talking about her business affairs, Katri had had a sense of unreality that often made it hard for her to re-establish the proper balance and significance of the numbers. Nevertheless, she would take the sums fairly won in this game and add them to previously recaptured sums, which by her reckoning already belonged to Mats. Then, with even more meticulous care, she would note down the percentages that fell to Anna.

But playing for pretend money upset her much more. Anna's way of juggling zeros was confusing, and for the first time in her life Katri lost track and sat in her room for long periods with her hands pressed on her eyes, trying to separate what was real from what was arbitrary play.

The numbers pursued her relentlessly, but they were no longer her allies. And Katri felt that Anna's game was a kind of punishment. The long-forgotten letters had been answered, and new ones arrived very rarely. Anna seemed disappointed. "Is there no one we can cheat today? Then let's play the millions game." The game allowed you to cow your opponent with percentages, and it didn't matter in the least whether you were bidding higher or lower.

They tried switching to auction piquet, but it was a mistake. Anna was a bad loser; it made her angry and snappish. They went back to the millions game.

* * *

On days when she was alone, Anna took the dog out in the back yard and had him retrieve. The dog had changed. When you passed him in the back hall, he could stand up and bare his teeth.

"Down," said Katri. And the dog would lie down.

23

A WHITE WROUGHT-IRON FLOWER TABLE ran beneath the window in Anna's bedroom. It had stood empty for a very long time. Katri wanted to use it to line up the folders containing Anna's private letters and the correspondence of Anna's parents. These folders were of white cloth to go with the furniture. "Oh, yes," Anna said. "Papa's and Mama's letters. I thought you'd put them out on the ice long ago. Did you read them too?"

Katri stiffened. Suddenly she saw how much Anna's face had changed. It had shrunk and acquired a touch of cunning that was not attractive. "No, I didn't read them," she said.

"Just think," said Anna. "Every year specified on the spine. Now I can look up anything I want, whenever I want, for example, a letter someone wrote to Papa in 1908."

Katri studied her face for a moment and then went her way without a word.

* * *

Anna wandered about the room, moving one piece of furniture after another, then moving them back again, and her ill humour pursued her until the need for comfort became overwhelming. Finally she took the white folder with Sylvia's letters and sat down on the edge of the bed.

The letters were in chronological order. She skipped the school years and Sylvia's marriage and all the postcards from Sylvia's Italian trip. Here were the condolence letters when Anna's parents died in rapid succession. Anna searched on impatiently; they had to come soon, the first watercolours. Here it was. "Dear Anna, how nice you have something to keep you busy. A little hobby always makes things easier."

No, not yet – they hadn't become important yet... only later, when Sylvia first saw them. Or when the first book came out, she couldn't remember... In any case, the first time they talked about Anna's work, really talked about it seriously, and Sylvia had said... She had helped Anna, somehow really helped her move on. Here maybe: "Life is short but art is long. Struggle on, little Anna." Or here: "Don't take it so seriously. Inspiration will come when it comes." Or: "I think your rabbits are really darling, so don't you worry about them."

In one of the last letters: "What do you mean when you say you want to preserve the landscape without misleading anyone? Did you get my little New Year's present..?"

Then the letters came at longer intervals and gradu-ally switched to Christmas cards. Anna searched back through earlier letters looking for the important passage, the decisive thing that Sylvia had said about her work, but it wasn't there. Sylvia hadn't understood and hadn't cared, and Sylvia was hopelessly sentimental.

Anna replaced the empty folder in its proper place and put the letters in a plastic bag. She went down to the cellar, put pieces of broken flowerpots into the bag, and tied it up tightly. Only the dog was at home. Anna put on warm clothes and took the path down to the shore. The ice was very slippery, and it was further than she'd realised out to the pile of furniture. It was a splendid rubbish pile, almost like a monument. She tried to distinguish and recognise items, but without success. She added her bag and turned for home. No one had seen her farewell to Sylvia. In the hall, she said to the dog, "Well, what do you say to that?" But this time without triumph. It was only an observation.

24

MATS SPENT HIS DAYS IN THE BOAT SHED and every evening after dinner he went up to his room. Katri asked no questions.

He's probably sitting and drawing, some detail or other that he wants to work on. He doesn't read any more, it's only the boat. Soon I'll need the down payment for Liljeberg, a third of the price. Next payment when it's planked and sided, and the final when it's finished. When I'm sure of the down payment, I can tell Mats it's his own boat he's building. But not yet. I don't dare talk to Anna yet, she's getting unpredictable. She could cheat, cancel Mats's percentage, say it had only been a game.

I need to wait and be very careful with her. Always wait. As far back as I can remember, I've done nothing but wait, wait to finally act, to wager all my insight and foresight and daring, wait for the big decisive change that sets everything right. The boat is very important, but it's only the beginning. I could double and triple her inheritance – dead money lying fallow – invest it wisely and bring it to life and give it back to her many times over in a millions game that isn't pretend any more, a game worthy of me. It can't be too late. It mustn't be too late!

25

ONE DAY WHEN KATRI WAS OUT WITH THE DOG, Anna opened her work drawer, the only one of all her cabinet drawers that was always impeccably tidy. It had been closed all winter. Anna carried out a ritual that she always repeated when the first spring fog rolled in from the sea. She lifted out the teak case with its worn, carefully oiled finish and conducted a painstaking examination of her paints. No additions needed. She tested the soft tips of her brushes, marten hair, the best brushes you could buy. She contemplated all her materials carefully, and everything was in order. She put everything back in precisely the same place. She went out into the woods behind the house and dug a hole in the snow. There was moss at the bottom. She pressed her hand against the frozen earth and felt how the ice was slowly beginning to melt. But the moment was not yet, not for some time to come.

26

KATRI WALKED OUT TOWARDS THE POINT. She could hear the first black grouse hooting and drumming at the edge of the woods. The ice was as grey as asphalt, and shadowy dark-blue clouds moved above it in long ribbons. The dog was uneasy and didn't keep pace. As they neared the lighthouse, he trotted away. She ordered him back in the very low tone that the dog knew and obeyed. He swung around sideways like a wolf, but he didn't come. Katri took out her cigarettes. Once again she ordered him back in an even lower voice, but the dog didn't move.

She turned away. The light was strong and transparent, the landscape seemed suffused with expectation. Along the shore, the ice had already broken up, and open water was breathing in the fissures, rising and spilling over the ice and falling back again. Katri lit a cigarette, crumpled the empty packet and threw it out on the ice. And the dog retrieved it, flung himself through the shore water, took it in his mouth and brought it back to her feet. With the hair on his back on end and his head on one side, he stared her straight in the eye, and Katri saw and understood that her dog had become an adversary. At home she went to Anna and said, "Anna, you've ruined my dog. You did it on the sly. I can't depend on him any more."

"Depend and depend," Anna shot back. "I don't know what you mean... Dogs like to play, don't they?!"

Katri walked to the window and, with her back to Anna, she went on. "You know perfectly well what you've done. The dog no longer knows what's expected of him. Is that so hard to grasp?"

"I don't understand!" Anna shouted. "Sometimes I'm supposed to play and sometimes not..."

"You don't play with a dog just for the fun of it. You know that."

"And what about you, Katri Kling? Your game about money isn't even fun. And don't go telling yourself that dog is happy. He just obeys..."

Katri turned around. "Obey?" she said. "You don't know the meaning of the word. It means believing in a person and following orders that are consistent, and it's a relief, it means freedom from responsibility. It's a simplification. You know what you have to do. It's safe and reassuring to believe in just one thing."

"Just one thing!" Anna burst out. "What a lecture. And why in the world should I obey you?"

Katri's reply was chilly. "I thought we were talking about the dog."

27

ONE MORNING ANNA DECLARED that she wanted to go to the shop and pick up her own mail.

"Do," Katri said. "But it's very slippery, so wear your leather boots, not the felt ones. And don't forget your sunglasses."

Anna took her felt boots. The hill was at its worst, and when she'd almost reached the road, she slipped and sat down in the snow. She looked quickly over her shoulder but all the windows were empty.

"Well, well," said the storekeeper. "So unusual to see you in the shop for once, Miss Aemelin. We were almost a little worried. I mean, we have no way of knowing what's going on at your place... Nowadays, I mean. What can I get for you?"

"I wanted some sweets, but I can't remember what they're called... It was such a long time ago. Something with kittens on it. Rectangular box with kittens."

"Kitty-Kitt," said the storekeeper caressingly. "It's an old brand. But we've got a new one, too, with puppies."

"No, thank you. The one with kittens."

"Very good. It can't be easy having such a big dog in the house. They say it's wild."

"The dog is very well behaved," said Anna guardedly. She recalled that the storekeeper had cheated her. His smile was not friendly, not even polite. Anna turned her back on him and walked over to the canned goods, but as usual it was impossible to decide what she really wanted. Fru Sundblom came in and greeted her with exaggerated amazement, bought coffee and macaroni, took a lemonade and sat down at the window table to listen.

The storekeeper said, "And Miss Kling has become such a marvellous housekeeper. Well, I've always said that she knows what she's doing. And her brother seems to be cleverer than we thought. Now they're building a boat that he designed. Isn't that right?"

"What's this?" Anna asked.

"That's yeast. People use it when they're baking bread."

Fru Sundblom cackled and poured herself more lemonade.

"Boats," the storekeeper resumed. "Boats are really wonderful things. I've always liked them. The boat is your commission, isn't it, Miss Aemelin?"

"No," Anna said. "I don't know a thing about boats, unfortunately. I read about them. This will be fine – please put it on my bill."

Suddenly the room seemed full of malice. As Anna was leaving, Fru Sundblom called after her. "Say hello to

Miss Kling. Please give my very special regards to Miss Kling!"

Anna walked home, forgetting to take her mail. What had they said? Just ordinary shop gossip... No. Oh, no, they couldn't fool her any more. She knew. They were venomous, inwardly they were sneering at her, Anna Aemelin, sneering at Katri and Mats... She would never go back. Never go anywhere, except into the woods. She needed to work, as quickly as possible... Right away...

The Kitty-Kitt didn't taste the way it had forty years ago and got stuck in her teeth in an unpleasant way. Anna walked faster, looking only down at the road. Several neighbours passed by, but she didn't notice their greetings, just wanted to get home, home to the dreadful Katri, to her own altered world which had grown severe but where nothing was wicked and concealed. At the end of the village street, Madame Nygård came towards her, placed herself in the middle of the street, and said, "Such a hurry we're in, Miss Aemelin! Are you out looking to see if spring is on its way? We'll be seeing the ground now pretty soon."

Her calm, friendly voice stopped Anna in her tracks. She stood in the slush and looked up, the spring sun burning her eyes.

"How's everything up at the rabbit house?"

"My, my," said Anna quickly. "Is that what you call it in the village?"

"Yes, indeed. Didn't you know?"

"No. No, I really didn't."

Madame Nygård looked earnestly at Anna and said, "But it's just a nickname. No one means any harm."

"Excuse me, I'm in something of a hurry," Anna said. "You wouldn't understand, but I'm very short of time just at the moment..."

The road was even icier closer to the shore. Her stick slipped, and it didn't help much to shuffle along with her legs wide and her toes turned out. It felt ridiculous. Anna climbed up in the snow beside the road to catch her breath, then went on. It wasn't much further now, but she grew steadily more anxious. She needed to get onto her own land as quickly as she could, in under her own wall of spruce where the snow was clean and unmarked by other people's tracks. At the bottom of the hill, the village children stood shouting something rhythmically, over and over the same thing, a single word that she couldn't make out. They were staring at her house.

"Don't shout!" Anna called at them. "I'm right here. What is it you want?"

The children stopped shouting and moved away.

"Now, don't be frightened," Anna said. "It was nice of you to come... But you see right at the moment I don't have time for you, I'm in a very great hurry..." She tried to find the bag of sweets in her purse. The children had lost interest in her, had turned towards the house and taken up their shouting again. It sounded like 'Witch, witch, witch...' Anna passed them and walked up the hill. The bag of sweets was sticky in her hands; she ripped it open and threw the sweets in the snow. "They're for you," she yelled, shaking her stick at them. Then she struggled on up the slippery hill.

A steady land breeze blew through the trees behind the house. The heavy new snow tumbled from spruce branches, first here, then there, filling the whole woods with steps and whispers. Between the tree roots on the sun side, the soil was showing dark and wet with little sprigs of lingon. Anna paused now and then as if waiting, and then walked on.

"She's out early this year," Liljeberg said, looking out of his window. "Maybe the old girl misread her calendar. And she's not as steady on her legs as she used to be."

"No wonder, with a witch in the house," his brother observed. "Gets to you eventually."

Edvard Liljeberg turned back into the room and said, "Now, you just hold your tongue. That witch you look down your nose at is ten times smarter than you are. And you're not that much nicer, either."

Anna walked along the edge of the woods, from tree to tree, the same route she took every year, with the same excitement, the accumulated anticipation of an entire winter. She recognised her forest floor, but today, this premature day, the black earth held no promise. It was just patches of wet soil that gave no hint, inspired no faith in coming miracles.

Anna went home.

28

ANNA ALWAYS THOUGHT OF HERSELF as a painter of the ground. She had said as much on several occasions and discovered to her surprise that her listeners took it as a sign of modesty. On the contrary, beneath this self-description was a quiet, sovereign conviction that she, Anna Aemelin, was, strictly speaking, the only person who could paint the forest floor in the one correct manner. And that this eternally living, growing forest floor could never fail her. But after her first visit to the woods, Anna was gripped by a terrible anxiety. Nothing and no one could have calmed her fears. She felt bereft and uprooted.

The day wore on and her anxiety grew. Anna hardly knew why she took out the letters Mama and Papa had received in the course of their long lives, but it had to do with her work, her relationship to her work. Somewhere in all these crowded folders there had to be an explanation, maybe a reference to when and why the child Anna or the little girl Anna had been captivated by the ground in the woods, had consecrated herself to this one thing that had never failed her, never until today. It was important. Someone, sometime, must have talked about her. There were many letters, far too many. But the people who had written to Julius and Elise Aemelin didn't mention their daughter. Anna went on reading, more and more rapidly, skimming, scanning. She wanted no supper, and when it got dark she lit the lamp and read on, making her way through a flood of words, messages, comments that had once had significance for these people long since dead, and with every folder she opened and then laid aside. Anna grew older, but no one mentioned her. At the most they wrote "Greetings to your daughter" or "Merry Christmas to all three of you". She didn't exist.

There was Papa's correspondence with government offices, his receipts for membership fees in clubs and societies, Mama's household accounts, rail tickets saved from trips abroad, postcards someone had sent from one of those Mediterranean places where people suddenly remember friends they never see, and "My dear Elise, congratulations on your daughter's graduation…" Later, condolences to Elise Aemelin, and then they stopped.

"Of course," Anna said. "Maybe that was when I started painting the ground."

29

THE NEXT MORNING, ANNA DIDN'T WANT TO GET UP. "Go away," she said.

"Aren't you feeling well?" Katri asked.

"It's nothing. I just don't want to."

Katri put the tea tray on the bed table. "That's the wrong book," Anna said. "I've read it. Anyway, it's so silly I didn't even bother to find out how it ended. They're all the same, the same things over and over again." And she put the pillow over her head and waited to be contradicted. But Katri went away. In the back hall, she stopped Mats on his way out and said, "Couldn't you go and talk to Anna for a while? She doesn't want to get up, and there's nothing wrong with her. She's just sulking."

"Why?" Mats said.

"I don't know."

"But what should I say?"

"Well, what do you talk about in the evening?"

"Not much," Mats said. "We talk about books."

"She doesn't read any more."

"I know. It's bad."

"And what is it that's so bad?"

Mats didn't answer, he just looked at his sister. When he went in to see Anna, he talked in general about getting boats in the water, how it wouldn't be long before the ice broke up.

"Listen, Mats," Anna said. "I realise you're here to comfort me, and Katri sent you."

"It's true."

"And it doesn't matter to me one whit when the boats go in the water."

"You're mistaken, Miss," said Mats earnestly. "It matters a great deal. And I can tell you that we're building a very beautiful boat at the moment."

"You don't say."

"And it's from my drawings." Mats paused in the doorway but couldn't come up with anything else to say. Finally, he asked if there was anything he could do.

"Yes, there is," Anna said. "You can take all this out on the ice. This house is getting so crowded I can hardly breathe!"

"But that would be a shame," Mats objected. "Those folders were expensive. Katri got white to match the furniture."

"Take them out," Anna said. "Carry them out to the furniture pile on the ice. They'll match just perfectly. And then it will all go down together. You said the ice was about to break up. I'd love to watch it all sink."

Anna didn't come to dinner, but later in the evening, when the house was dark, she went to the kitchen to find something nice in the refrigerator. And she'd hardly started rummaging through Katri's plastic containers when Mats appeared in the doorway and said, "Hi."

"So there you are again," Anna said. "Just look how your sister has organised this food! No one could possibly know what's in these without opening every one of the wretched things... Did you take it out on the ice?"

"Yes, I did. But if you want anything more out there, you'll have to hurry. The ice could go any time."

"I'm looking for cheese. But why cheese should be in plastic I can't imagine. Do you think it will sink?"

"Most of it. But some of it will float around for a while before it does."

"You know, Mats, sometimes I get so tired without any reason. What was it you were saying about the plans for that boat?"

"Just that they're my drawings."

"I'd like to look at them."

"But the best ones are down at the boat shed. I've only got the sketches."

"Bring them here."

"But they're not that good. They're very rough."

"Mats," Anna said. "Go get them. This will probably be the only time in your life you'll get a chance to show your sketches to someone who really understands the concept 'sketch'."

Anna sat and studied the drawings for a long time, going through all of them. Finally she said, "That line is good."

"It's called the sheer," Mats said.

Anna nodded. "It's a good word. Did you ever stop to think how often the terminology of work is beautiful and expressive and still matter-of-fact? You know, the names of things, the names of tools, the names of colours?"

Mats smiled at Anna. In drawing after drawing, she saw the line feeling its way stubbornly, patiently, searchingly towards its final arc of suppressed energy, and suddenly for the first time she saw the snowdrift out on the veranda. It was the same curve. "I think your boat will be beautiful," she said.

Mats started to explain. With a stream of words, he tried to give Anna an education about the seaworthiness and bearing capacity of boats. He made no attempt to avoid the technical terminology she had never heard, but Anna did not break her attentive silence by asking questions. Finally, Mats leaned back in his chair, stretched his arms straight above his head and laughed. "Twenty horsepower!" he said. "Straight out! All the way!"

"Yes," Anna said. "All the way out. Now I see why you don't care about reading old sea stories any more, not now, while you're building your own boat."

"But it's not mine," Mats said.

"It's not your boat?"

"No, only the drawings are mine. They're going to sell the boat."

"And who's going to buy it?"

"I don't think the Liljebergs know yet. They're just building it." He stood up and rolled up his papers.

"Wait a moment," Anna said. "If you had your own boat... What would you do?"

"Take it out, of course. And stay away for days."

"Alone?"

"You bet."

"I used to long for a boat," Anna said. "A boat of my own at the shore so I could go off whenever I wanted. Without them knowing, the others... I imagined a white rowing boat. Can you run a motor?"

"I'm learning," Mats said.

The garden door opened and closed again. They waited. They heard Katri walk down the hall.

"Is it hard to learn?" Anna asked.

"Not if you want to. When we've got the boat launched and moored, we'll do the final inspection. And then it's time to think about the motor housing and the petrol tanks and the seats. And the cabin. All that stuff comes later. The main thing is getting the boat out of the way to make room in the shed for the next job."

Anna was only half listening. "I used to row," she said. "I'd borrow a dory and row off by myself, but the islands were too far out, and then there was always the problem of getting back in time for dinner... But if I buy this boat you designed, you mustn't think I'd want to ride around in it all the time. I'll probably use it very rarely. Actually, I only need to know it's there... Just the idea of it, you know. You must never forget that it's yours."

"I don't understand," Mats said.

"What is it you don't understand?"

Mats just shook his head and looked at her, almost sternly.

"You think I'm just talking," said Anna impatiently. "You don't know that, if there's something I really want, then I get it, all the way, and nothing stops me. It's a shame I so seldom really want anything these days... But I want to give you this boat. No, we're not going to talk about it any more, not now. And it's to be a secret, just between us. Now I'm going to bed. And I'm going to sleep very well and very long."

30

"HAVE YOU GOT A MINUTE?" Mats asked. Liljeberg looked up from his work and saw it was private. They walked to one side of the shed.

"What is it?"

"You haven't promised the boat to anyone, have you?"

"We'll see what happens."

"Because it's mine," Mats whispered. "You understand, it's my boat. I'm going to be its owner."

"You don't say. And how did you plan to pay for it? Is that all set?"

"It's all set."

"So, it worked out after all," said Liljeberg amiably. "Don't worry, we haven't promised the boat to the wrong person, not at all. The important thing is that I know what to tell the others. An anonymous donor – that sounds good. Just so long as it's all set."

Later that day, Liljeberg was standing outside the boat shed smoking when Katri came by on the road. "Hi, little witch," he said. "So things are starting to fall into place."

Katri and the dog stopped. She liked Liljeberg.

"Everything seems to be working out," he said. "And there's no hurry about that down payment. Anyway, it's nice not having to go around pretending any more. Now everyone knows it's Mats's boat."

Katri froze. "Who said so?"

"Mats himself, of course. He told me it was all set. Is something wrong?"

"No."

"You look tired," Liljeberg said. "You shouldn't take life so seriously. Things have a way of working out if you just wait."

"They do not. Nothing works out just by waiting. And sometimes you wait too long." Katri walked on, the dog lagging behind. Liljeberg stood watching them, thinking that something wasn't right.

Katri walked out towards the point. Quietly, in a very deep voice, she gave repeated commands to the dog. The dog ran to one side, the hair on his shoulders standing straight up, his ears pointing forwards as if in attack. Suddenly Katri lost her calm and screamed at him. She just stood in the road and screamed at the dog, screamed at the whole world, at all the things she hadn't the strength for, unrestrained words that sprang from disappointment and exhaustion. And the dog started barking. No one in the village had ever heard Katri's dog bark. They were used to the yapping of mongrels, but this was the barking of a large wolfhound, and they heard it everywhere and wondered what had happened. The dog continued to bark. Slowly he followed Katri to the house. She tied him up in the yard, and he went right on barking.

"What's wrong with your dog?" Anna said. "Why is he barking?"

"He's not my dog any more," Katri said. "You've taken him from me. And what have you done with Mats? You sat there night after night, whispering across your books, planning and making your deals..."

"What are you talking about? I don't know what you're talking about..."

"The boat! His boat! You've given it to him." Katri came closer. She was crying silently, her face rigid. "You gave him the boat," she said. "It was supposed to come from me. You must have known that."

"No," Anna burst out. "No, I didn't know!"

"The Mats Game! For me it was serious."

"I didn't know," Anna repeated. "Don't be this way. You frighten me..."

"I know," Katri said. "We have to take care of you. You're so sensitive. You despise money. It means nothing to you, you give it away, you sit on it, you play with it, and, no matter what you do, we have to take care of you. Anna. It's so much fun to give a present, isn't it? To someone nice who's surprised and grateful? I've lived with him my whole life, and waited all that time to make him happy. Everything's written down. It's all noted down in clear, honest numbers that you've approved yourself. Isn't that true? I had an idea..."

Anna was very frightened, and from the depths of her incomprehension she cried, "You know nothing about ideas! Mats knows. I know. We try to shape them, but all you do is arithmetic... Go away."

Katri didn't answer.

"I had one idea," Anna said. "I did. But not any more. Can't you make your dog be quiet?"

* * *

Oh, Anna, let the dog bark, let him howl out my lament for caprice and self-deception, for gentle, unconscious cruelty and easy, narrow-minded evasion and stupidity – most of all stupidity, talented, incurable stupidity. Howl it out to the heavens! Because you will never know and never understand what I've tried to do!

* * *

Katri walked down to the shore, where Mats was walking towards her. "Why is the dog barking?" he asked.

She didn't answer.

"Something must be wrong with him. What are you going to do?"

"Nothing."

"Nothing? What do you mean? You know you're the only one he's got."

"Mats, please," Katri said. "Don't be angry. Not right now."

"But it's like you didn't care."

She shook her head. Neither of them spoke, and then she said, "Look at the rocks out there. They look like flowers, don't they?" They looked at the big rocks along the shore that now in the spring stuck up pitch-black against the receding ice. Around each of them the ice had ruptured up like huge flower petals. Katri was right: the rocks really did look like flowers, dark blossoms extending far out from the shoreline and casting long shadows across the ice. The sun, about to set, rolled out an avenue of shimmering gold right to their feet.

"Katri," Mats said. "Come. I want to show you something. But you have to hurry, we've only got a few minutes."

The evening sun was just as strong inside the boat shed, shining at them from every polished surface, every tiny tool, so that the whole room sparkled like dark gold, brimming with sunset and calm. Katri looked at the boat. It was under construction, still only a skeleton, a lattice-work, and it shone most clearly of all. And then the sun sank below the horizon and the colours died.

"Thank you," Katri said. "Would it be all right if I stayed for a while? I know, I need to let myself out on the water side."

"Yes, that's best," Mats said. "And don't forget to close the latch."

31

THE DOG BARKED ALL NIGHT. Sometimes he howled. Towards morning, Katri went out, turned him loose, and he ran into the woods. Later, the barking resumed far away.

The next day the dog killed a rabbit – actually an insignificant event, just one of the Liljebergs' rabbits killed by a dog instead of having its neck wrung a day or two later as planned. They had sat down to dinner. The dog scratched at the hall door, Mats let him in, and he ran in to Anna and laid the dead rabbit at her feet. Anna dropped her spoon in her soup and went pale.

"Take it out," Katri said. "Mats. Quickly."

Anna sat still, staring at the floor. There wasn't much blood, just a few drops. Katri got up, dropped her napkin on the unhappy bloodstains, walked over to Anna and said, "It's nothing. This is nothing to get upset about."

"Maybe not," Anna observed and went on slowly eating her soup. "Go and sit down." After a few moments, she added, "Katri, you are kind to me."

The dead rabbit was thrown out onto the ice.

32

THE DOG CONTINUED TO BARK at night, sometimes far away, sometimes close to the house. Towards morning, he would howl. It could be quiet for hours, but there were those who lay in bed waiting for the next howl, and they would say, "Did you hear that? It's like having a wolf in the woods. An unhappy woman has an unhappy dog. It ought to be shot."

Katri did not talk about the dog, but she put out food and water in the yard. Sometimes at night Mats would wait by the kitchen window with the light off and the door open. He saw the dog only once, just as it was growing light, and he went very slowly out on the steps and tried to coax it in. But it ran off into the woods, so he gave up.

One Sunday, Madame Nygård came to visit. She had baked, and the bread she brought was still warm, wrapped in a towel. "Miss Aemelin," she said, "I would like to speak to you alone, if Katri doesn't mind. As I under-stand it, you are in the habit of sitting at table together."

She came quickly to the point. "I am older than you, Miss Aemelin, and therefore I venture to speak of things that might otherwise be left unsaid. People in the village are talking. And I thought it would be just as well to come up and enquire as to just what is going on here in the rabbit house."

"What do they say?" Anna said quickly. "What are they saying about me? Is it the storekeeper?"

"Now my dear, please, let's not get excited..."

"Oh, I know it is," Anna interrupted. "He's the one. It's him. He's an evil man, not to be trusted." Clearly defined red spots had suddenly appeared on Anna's cheeks, and her eyes were sharp as she leaned towards her guest. "It's true – admit it, it's him. Or else Liljeberg. They cheat. They cheat Mats. Mats has been underpaid the whole time, everyone knows it. And it's all about the boat, isn't it?"

Madame Nygård was silent for a long time. Finally she said, gravely, "I had a feeling that all was not well up here, and now I know I was right. Listen to me now, my dear little friend. We just want to know if you're all right. Why is that dog howling?"

Anna pushed her coffee cup away. "Excuse me," she said. "I've never really liked coffee. I used to like it. I mean, I used to think I liked it... I don't know. I don't know why it howls. I don't want to talk about this."

"Miss Anna, is the boat a gift from you?"

"No, it's Katri's gift."

"Oh yes, Katri. Yes, she's been squirrelling it away for quite some time."

"And what if she has?" Anna exclaimed defiantly. "Katri's been saving her money for a long time, and she has everything written down in a notebook!"

Madame Nygård nodded slowly. "Yes, indeed," she said. "It's not everyone has such a good head on their shoulders."

"Katri is honest!" Anna went on vehemently. "She's the only one I can depend on!"

"But why are you getting so excited? We all know that Katri Kling is a capable and conscientious young woman. My dear little Anna..."

Anna interrupted again. "Don't say 'my dear little...' Wait. Wait a moment, it's nothing..." After a little while, she explained that it was just age, her eyes teared so easily... "And the spring sun. A little more coffee?"

"No, thank you. No more for me."

Madame Nygård sat quietly waiting with her hands clasped on her stomach. Finally Anna took up the conversation to speak about something that had been bothering her for quite some time – the fact that she had begun speaking ill of people. "I never used to do that," she said. "Believe me, I never did. Someone came to Mama once and said, 'Your daughter is unusual; she never speaks ill of anyone.' I remember it, I remember it quite clearly. But why? Did I trust everyone? Or was it only that I forgave them?"

"Well, well," said Madame Nygård. "That snow fell a long time ago, did it not?"

"But you trust people, don't you?"

"Yes, I suppose I do. Why shouldn't I? One sees and hears a great deal about the way people behave, but that's their problem. One doesn't want to make things worse by not believing that they mean what they say."

"It's beginning to get dark," Anna said. "I don't want to keep you too long."

"I'm in no hurry," said Madame Nygård. "Those days are over. But I think I should be going in any case. Sometimes it's not wise to say too much all at once."

That night the dog stopped howling.

33

SPRING CAME CLOSER. During the day, the soil under the trees steamed in the warm sun; the nights were ice cold and deep blue. It was a brilliantly beautiful time. The boat was almost ready to be launched, but no one talked about it at the rabbit house. The eiders had arrived. One night, the wind began blowing in from the sea. Katri lay listening, remembering the spring nights when she used to go down to the water to wait for the ice to break up. She'd been very young. And when it came time for the first seagulls, she used to go out to wait for them. They almost always came the same night every year.

Yes, they always came at night. I'd stand and freeze and listen, and I was completely alone with the landscape and the night, and even then I had the patience I have now. And my thoughts were as grand back then as they are now – plans and conquests out in the wide world – but they were thoughts without a foothold or a clear goal. They were just powerful. Now I know what I want.

Katri couldn't sleep. At dawn she got up, dressed, and went outdoors. It wasn't cold, and the wind was strong and steady. The sun was ready to come up, and the same gentle, transparent, colourless light lay across the shore and the ice and the sky. Katri stood at the end of the fish pier and watched the dark ice bulge and bend over the swells moving in towards the shore, a long, slow, rising and sinking surge.

It'll break, but not yet. Ice is tough. There must be open water further out. They'll be putting boats in the water soon. Why doesn't he say anything about the boat?

Katri walked on towards the lighthouse point. Halfway out she caught sight of the dog, following her at the edge of the woods, sometimes hidden by the trees. When she reached the lighthouse, he had disappeared. Katri climbed the steps to the locked lighthouse door, the sun straight in her eyes. Right at the shoreline, the ice had broken up. Thin floes rustled and whispered as they bumped against the rocks, piled up and broke apart. The water was very dark.

The attack was silent, but Katri sensed the dog's ferocity and murderous intent, and she threw herself back against the wall of the lighthouse and flung her arms in front of her face. The dog's leap was grand, worthy of a large animal that had never used his strength to the uttermost, and for a moment his breath was hot on her throat. His claws scraped against the cement as his heavy body fell backwards. They stood still, looking at each other, and both their eyes were yellow. Finally, the dog laid his ears back and dropped his tail. Then suddenly flung himself around and ran east, away from the village.

* * *

Mats was in the back yard piling wood when Katri came home. Right away he said, "What's happened."

"Nothing,"

"Who ripped your coat?"

"The dog. But he missed. Nothing happened."

Mats walked towards her. "You keep saying 'Nothing happened.' What happened with the dog?"

"He ran off."

"This is bad. Now he'll probably never come back. He'll go wild. He won't survive. And you just keep saying nothing happened."

"Let it go," Katri said. "What do you want me to do?"

"Care!" he yelled. "You have to care! He's your dog. You scare him."

"Mats, you're repeating yourself," Katri said. "You've been spending too much time with Anna. Take care, she's not good for you right at the moment." And then Katri couldn't stop herself. She started screaming at her beloved brother. "What is it you're thinking? What do you think's going on? Haven't I tried? I made an honourable deal. I've tried to give protection, I've given security where there was no security, no direction, nothing! I provide safety. What are you thinking? Haven't you seen the way I walked through the village with that dog, side by side like one superior creature? That dog was as confident and proud as a king! Every one of those mongrels went silent when we walked by. We could count on each other – we never left each other in the lurch, we were one, a unit, and I expected..."

"What did you expect?"

"I don't know," she said. "Maybe that you'd all believe in me, trust me... When you finish that woodpile, remember to cover it. Use that sheet metal behind the shed."

In the back hall, Katri rolled up her coat and placed it at the back of the cubby-hole where the Aemelins stored their winter boots.

34

THE NIGHTS HAD ALREADY GROWN BRIGHT and with every day that passed the nights grew shorter. Katri couldn't sleep. Finally she hung a blanket over the window, but it didn't help a bit. She knew the spring night was out there. Sleep and darkness go together. Bright nights are wakeful and uneasy.

Why was Mats so angry with me? Doesn't he understand? He must understand how hard I try, all the time, to put everything I do to a strict test – every act, every word I choose instead of a different word. If you try with all your power to the utmost, shouldn't it then be your motives that matter most? Shouldn't they count for more than the final result? If you do everything you can to take responsibility, to offer protection, and you don't give personal convenience the tiniest leeway..? Dependent people need to be left alone to absolutely rely on and believe in the person who makes decisions for them and teaches them and gives them guidance and security... Everyone ought to understand that...

And where is the dog, where's he run to tonight? He doesn't believe in anyone any more, so he's become as dangerous as a wolf. But wolves do better, they run in packs; it's only solitary animals that get chased away or slain...

Katri went out in the yard. The dog had not been there, his food was untouched. There was a light in the kitchen. Anna threw up the window and called, "Katri? Is that you? Where did you put what was left of the meatballs?"

"At the bottom, on the right. It's a square plastic container."

"So you can't sleep, either," Anna said.

"No. It takes time to get used to these bright nights."

"I used to like it," Anna said. "I used to like a lot of things." Her voice was cold.

"When you were young."

"Not then," Anna said. "Not so long ago. For that matter, I don't want anything to eat, and you can bring in the dog dish. He isn't coming back. He wants to get away from you." Anna turned off the light in the kitchen. In the parlour, the night brightness was strong in all the windows facing the sea.

Behind her, Katri said, "Anna? Wait a moment – don't go yet. Couldn't you please tell me what it is that's happened to you?" When Anna didn't answer, Katri went on. "Don't you know what I'm talking about?"

"Oh yes, I know," Anna replied, and her voice was altered; it was a voice of compassion. "I know what you're talking about. What's happened to me is that I can no longer see the ground." And Anna went into her room and closed the door.

35

ONE BEAUTIFUL, QUIET SPRING MORNING Mats came in and said, "Now you can come and see. We've cleaned up the shed and we're not working today." He was very happy. On the way down to the harbour, he explained to Katri and Anna that the Liljebergs never showed half-finished work; not even the buyer was allowed into the shed until the boat was ready for launching. "Of course, drawings are another matter. They'll go over them with you as many times as you like, but then you have to let them build it. That's the difference between the craftsman and the buyer."

When they entered the boat shed, the Liljeberg brothers, standing by the workbench, greeted them with reserved politeness and left Mats to do the presentation. He was young and eager and had not yet discovered the silence of the proud professional. The floor had been swept, and every tool hung in its rack. The boat stood by itself in the middle of the shed, signed with the pretentious 'W' for 'Wästerby'. Mats's explanations were rapid and quiet. He went through all the technical features, led Katri and Anna around the boat, drawing their attention to details that had taken much thought and been difficult to achieve. The women said little, listened earnestly, nodded from time to time the way one does for a fine piece of work. Finally Mats stopped talking and they stood quietly by the sternpost.

"Well, well," said Edvard Liljeberg, walking over to them. "So now you've seen all of her and we're all set. We'll be launching her soon. Now there's just one important matter to attend to – namely, the christening. What are you going to call her?"

No one spoke. Finally Anna put her hand on the sternpost and said, "We can call her 'Katri'. That's a good name for a boat. And anyway, it is Katri's gift to Mats."

"That sounds fine," Edvard said. "So we can drink a toast to her when the time comes." His brothers walked over and shook hands, and they began a general discussion about where they should put the name, on the stern or the bow or maybe on the side of the cabin, either in brass letters or carved into the wood. Suddenly Anna said, "But where's Katri?"

"Maybe she left," said one of the Liljeberg brothers, thinking she might at least have said goodbye. Getting your name on a boat doesn't happen every day.

Edvard said, "So let's leave it at that and take the rest of the day off. If everyone's satisfied, then I'm certainly happy."

Anna and Mats walked home. The hill up to the house was muddy and full of rivulets.

"Let me hold on to you," Anna said. "This hill is just as bad every year. Worse."

"There's something I don't understand," said Mats hesitantly. "That evening we talked about the boat, Miss Aemelin, and you said..."

Anna interrupted. "Yes, yes, I say a lot of things. I was wrong. Your sister's been saving up for that boat for a very long time, so she could give it to you. And, moreover, I'm not Miss Aemelin, I'm Anna. Now just stop worrying about things. Just figure out how you want the bunks and the engine box and whatever comes after that."

* * *

Katri saw the boat model as soon as she came into her room. Mats had put it in the window, where it was silhouetted against the sky. Katri closed the door, walked over, and saw that it was an exact copy down to the last detail. Mats must have worked on it for a long time. He had used the same woods. There were bunks, an engine box, a painter, everything. The fittings were brass. The name was engraved on the bow with careful attention to the classic calligraphic conventions. The name was Katri.

* * *

They had come home. Anna went into her room. Mats came up the stairs. Katri heard him coming and immediately wanted to go out to him but she was embarrassed and couldn't move and didn't know what to say. Just before he closed his door, her hesitation broke and she ran out and took him in her arms, only for an instant, and neither of them spoke. It was the first time Katri had ever dared embrace him.

* * *

Towards afternoon the wind died and it grew very quiet, just occasional dog yelps from the village. And not a sound had come from Anna's room all day.

I know, she's gone to bed again. She gets under the coverlet and sleeps her time away because she no longer sees the ground, so there's nothing at all she wants to do. She weighs me down to the earth; she's there all the time like a weight; she, Anna Aemelin. I remember the dog at home, when I was a girl; the one that killed chickens. They tied a dead hen around his neck and he carried it around with him all day until he just lay there unmoving with his eyes shut in a morass of shame. It was cruel. There's nothing so hideously easy as giving someone a bad conscience... Will it go on like this? Probably. Does she think she's the only one who's tired, hiding there under her coverlet, giving up because the world isn't the way she imagined it? Is it my fault!? How long does a person have a right to go around with blinders – what does she expect, this Anna Aemelin... what more does she want me to do? If she really were what she pretends to be, everything would have been wrong, everything I did and said and tried to get her to see, it would all have been monstrous. But her innocence left her a very long time ago, and she never noticed. She eats only grass, but she has a meat eater's heart. And she doesn't know it, and no one has told her. Maybe they don't care enough about her to take the chance. What should I do? How many different truths are there, and what justifies them? What a person believes? What a person accomplishes? Self-deception? Is it only the result that counts? I no longer know.

Anna's cane rapped on the ceiling, several times, angrily. When Katri went down to her, she was sitting in her bed wrapped tightly in her coverlet. "What are you doing up there?" she said. "You've been clumping back and forth for hours! I'm trying to sleep."

"I know," Katri said. "It's all you do. You sleep and sleep. Do you think it's easy for me, knowing you're sleeping your days away because nothing is exactly the way you'd imagined?"

"What do you mean?" Anna said. "What have you found to preach about now? I never get any peace in this house. Aren't you happy about his boat?"

"Yes, Anna, I am happy about his boat. It was very noble of you. Or, rather, it was simply fair of you."

"Whatever you say," said Anna irritably. "And what's wrong with my wanting to sleep? Anyway, now you've woken me up completely. Sit down and get a grip on yourself. What is the problem?"

"There's something I need to tell you. It's important."

"If it's United Rubber now, again..." Anna began.

"No. It's important. Listen to me. Listen carefully. I haven't been honest with you. You need to know that

I've lied right from the outset. I've told you things that aren't true about other people. I was wrong, and now I need to tell you. It can't be helped, but it needs to be said." Katri spoke very quickly. She stood in the door and looked past Anna at the wall.

"Remarkable," Anna said. "Really remarkable." She stood up and smoothed her dress and put the coverlet back in place. "You're amazing. Sometimes I think you're the world's most deadly serious person. Other people talk, you make pronouncements. The only entertaining thing about you is that all of a sudden you say something totally unexpected. Are you being entertaining now?"

"No," said Katri without a smile.

"Can you repeat all those things you just said?"

"No."

"You said you've been telling me stories."

"Yes."

"And what does that mean?"

"It means..." said Katri with difficulty. "It means that those people weren't cheating you. By 'those people', I mean the people you deal with. The people around you, and the people who write to you. They haven't cheated you. You can trust them again."

"Take a cigarette and sit down," Anna said. "Don't stand there looking like that. There's the ashtray. Are you speaking now about the storekeeper, for example, and Liljeberg?"

"Yes."

"Or perhaps our terrible Fru Sundblom?" Anna said, and laughed.

"Anna, this is serious. It's very important."

But Anna went on, suddenly in wicked high spirits. "Important? What do you mean by 'important'? Maybe 'meaningful'? Are you talking about the plastics companies? You mean they weren't cheating me after all? They were as nice as my publishers? They were just as innocent as all those depraved children who only wanted to take and take and take..? Is that what you're trying to tell me?"

"Anna, please."

"They weren't cheating me? None of them?"

"None of them."

"You are a very strange person," Anna said. "You lay out your calculations and your proofs. You find evil in everyone and get me to believe you. And then you come to me and say, you dare to come to me and say that none of it was true? Why are you doing this?"

They had been sitting in chairs on opposite sides of the little table that stood against the wall. Anna stared at Katri, and it suddenly seemed to her that she had never seen a sadder human being than Katri Kling. "Are you trying to be nice to me?" she asked.

"Now you're suspicious," Katri said. "But there's one thing you can believe. I never try to be nice. I'll repeat what I said until you believe me."

"But then I can never believe you again?"

"No. You can't."

Anna leaned across the table and said, "Katri, there is something about you that's too..." she searched for the word "... absolute. And it leads nowhere. Wouldn't it be a good idea for you to go and lie down for a while?" She put her hand on Katri's. "Just for an hour or two. Then maybe we can make sense of all this."

"Too absolute?" Katri said. "And it leads nowhere?" She put out her cigarette. "If anyone is absolute, it's you. And it leads straight where you want it to lead. I know it. I'll write you a letter."

"No more letters..."

"Just the one. And you're not allowed to stuff it in your cupboard. I'll prove to you that I was wrong. You said so yourself. I can calculate and I can prove. You'll be convinced right down to the last detail that I was wrong."

"Katri," Anna said. "Couldn't you go and take a little nap? It's been a long day."

"Yes," Katri said. "It has been long. I'll go."

36

WHEN KATRI RETURNED TO HER ROOM, she pulled her suitcase out from under the bed. She opened it, then just sat on the edge of the mattress and listened. The evening was very quiet. But the tranquil silence gave her no help in deciding what she had to do. Words and pictures – unspoken or hasty words, unseen or overly explicit pictures – tumbled through her mind and the only image that ultimately stuck was the dog, a dog running on and on without rest under the ominous ensign of the wolf skin.

37

ONE IMPORTANT AND CAREFULLY CONSIDERED morning, Anna went out very early to work. She had picked the spot the day before and carried out a stool low enough to sit on and still have her paintbox and her water cup within reach. Anna didn't use an easel. Easels seemed to her an altogether too assertive aid, too obvious. She liked to work as unobtrusively as possible, the paper spread on a board in her lap, close to her hand. The light is best in the morning, or in the evening when the colours deepen, and one has to work fast before the shadows fade and vanish.

Anna sat and waited for the morning mist to draw off through the woods. The silence she needed was complete. And when every bothersome element had departed, the forest floor emerged, moist and dark and ready to burst with all the things waiting to grow. Cluttering the ground with flowery rabbits would have been unthinkable.

TITLES IN SERIES

For a complete list of titles, visit www.nyrb.com or write to:
Catalog Requests, NYRB, 435 Hudson Street, New York, NY 10014